Richard Carpenter's

ROBIN OF SHERWOOD

THE MAGIC MAN

Richard Carpenter's
Robin of Sherwood
The Magic Man
By Jennifer Ash
Published in 2025 by
Chinbeard Books

in association with
Oak Tree Books
oaktreebooks.uk

Original *Robin of Sherwood*
television series copyright ©
1983 HTV/Goldcrest Films & TV.

Editor: Barnaby Eaton-Jones
Sub Editor: Harriet Whitehouse

Inspired by a story
by Barnaby Eaton-Jones

Cover art by by Barnaby
Eaton-Jones and Robert Hammond
Cover shows a depiction of *the Magic Man*

Richard Carpenter's

ROBIN OF SHERWOOD

THE MAGIC MAN

by
Jennifer Ash

A Chinbeard Books / Oak Tree Books Original

For Kip

This story is set after *The King's Fool*
and before *The Prophecy*

PROLOGUE

Rain fell like arrows on a battlefield, thick and fast. It would have driven even the hardiest soul undercover. But here, deep within the northern-most mountains of Wales, there were no huts or cottages within which to shelter, no workshops in which to labour. No souls.

Except one.

The druid, Elis, stood by the fire that spluttered in the centre of a crevice in the rock that he'd made into his home, a cramped dwelling which had been formed with the help of a rock fall, stubborn strength and sorcery.

Upon the fire sat a wide-open bowl made from stone; within that, a sapphire-blue liquid bubbled and frothed.

Staring into the bowl, he silently mouthed out the spell he was creating. Snatching up a willow twig from where it was resting against the stone wall, Elis stirred it through the liquid and held his breath.

A moment later, he let out a sigh.

Finally.

He'd found him. The man who'd denied his people—the Fferyllt—their collective survival so many years ago.

'He had no right to withhold his power from us,' the bitter words slipping from his tongue as he watched the picture forming in the blue liquid. His old enemy was running through a forest—*an English forest...*

'One mind—*his* mind—was all we needed to keep going. To become *invincible.*'

Elis let out a ragged cough, but ignored how much his chest ached. If he dwelt upon the pain that raged inside, his waning strength might fail him. Lowering the twig, the druid whispered the incantation he'd had prepared for so long—an enchantment which would allow him access to his enemy's mind.

'See what is beyond your sight... follow the visions... follow them to me. Listen to my voice... do as I say... hear me hidden beneath other's voices.

Help those who need help… and then betray them. Follow the visions… follow them to me…'

Elis saw the man blink in confusion as he suddenly faltered in his stride. The druid watched as the figure searched around himself, as if hunting for something that troubled him. Then, suddenly, a breeze stirred fast in the trees and a shadow fell across the scene, obscuring his vision.

The druid leant forwards, unsure as to what had happened—but the picture in the bowl had already changed.

His enemy had gone.

An angry curse formed on the druid's lips, but the words froze before they were spoken… for he could see another man; this one was younger and more purposeful, with an arrogant gleam to his eyes… and he was coming this way.

A smile crossed Elis's face for the first time in years. Decades, even.

This man was physically strong. He had to be to survive the mountains he was scaling while wearing such inadequate clothing.

This was a man he could use.

CHAPTER ONE

The sunset was stunning. It radiated an orange glow that felt full of hope and yet was, at the same time, heartbreakingly sad; it heralded the end of another day in the waking world.

Standing in the gatehouse of his monastic home, Abbot Hugo found himself fleetingly touched as he took in the majesty of the fading of the light. Any chance he might have had to savour the wonder of his God's creation was destroyed as soon as it began however, as the sound of a familiar footfall reached his ears.

Robert de Rainault, Sheriff of Nottingham, strode through the door of the gatehouse and ex-claimed, 'Honestly, Hugo, you become less Christian by the day!'

4

With barely contained contempt, the Abbot sniped back, 'Well, you would know all about that, Robert.'

'Gisburne and I came here to check on the food supplies for the abbey and the castle, yet you've shared nothing more with us than a dreary plate of pork since we arrived.'

The abbot tutted loudly, 'I'm amazed either of you even noticed the pork. Especially you, Robert... as you were making serious headway into the dwindling supplies of claret.'

'It's my claret!'

'It's the abbey's claret, actually.'

Sir Guy of Gisburne joined his two superiors just in time to hear the latest round in a battle of non-stop bickering that had been going on since Hugo had had the audacity to be born and disrupt his older brother's life.

'It was my idea to bring the tithe of food we took from the villages here for storage. And just because it's on Church land, that doesn't stop it from being my food! Anyway, you have far more food in your larder here than we have at the castle. It's not right. I'm the sheriff, and you're merely a cleric! You're supposed to embrace suffering, for God's sake,' complained the Sheriff.

'Exactly, Robert. What we do here IS for God's sake.'

Almost choking on the hypocrisy, the elder de Rainault poked a finger at his brother's purple robes. 'And yet, as I have just pointed out, somehow your larder always seems to be better stocked than mine.'

'It's hardly my fault if the people from the surrounding villages offer food in return for my blessings. Nor is it my fault that you allowed the rats to get into your store and consume your supplies!'

'I hardly allowed them to—'

Hugo elevated his voice, shouting over his brother. 'If you hadn't been so careless with the vermin, then you wouldn't have needed to take more from the people, would you?'

'But, Hugo, as a man of God, you are supposed to share—especially with your own brother!'

Hugo gave his head a sharp shake. 'The last harvest was only just the right side of poor. You know how fast supplies can become scarce if care isn't taken to manage them properly. I am keeping hold of what we have here. The brothers of Saint Mary's do need feeding, you know. It's alright for you; you only have yourself to feed.'

'And Gisburne, dozens of servants and—'

Hugo shook his head. 'I've no food to spare, so stop your bleating.'

'Hmmm…' The Sheriff shot his brother a filthy look before whipping around to face his deputy. 'Get the horses, Gisburne.'

'Already in hand, my Lord,' Sir Guy said as he pointed across the courtyard. 'I've instructed the men to have them waiting for us outside.'

'That's unusually organised of you, Gisburne.' The Sheriff gave him a suspicious look.

'The sun will be fully set soon, my Lord. We should return to the castle before nightfall.'

'Scared of riding through Sherwood in the dark, Gisburne?'

'No, my Lord Sheriff, but *you* are, so we should go.'

Chuckling, the abbot strode forwards. 'I'll walk with you as far as the outer gateway, Robert.'

Not appreciating being teased, an unusually taciturn Sheriff followed Hugo, keeping his eyes averted from the knowing smile he knew would be playing on Gisburne's lips.

Under the shadow of the trees that lined one side of the road that led from St Mary's Abbey to Nottingham, Hugo helped heave his brother onto the saddle of his mare, as Gisburne leapt astride his black stallion.

'This matter is not closed,' the Sheriff said as he gathered his reins. 'The castle requires more food, Hugo. That was the point of our additional tithe in the first place. I know you have more than enough for yourself and a bunch of monks. I want my share, and I shall have it.'

Not bothering to reply, the Abbot turned to leave. He'd only taken two strides towards his home, however, when a bedraggled figure stumbled out from between the trees.

'Dear God!' exclaimed Hugo, staggering backwards to collide with his brother's horse. The mare—startled by both newcomer and Abbot—reared up, depositing its rider into a nearby bush.

The Sheriff's furious yell of shock was overshadowed only by the sound of his men-at-arms battling to control their own frightened horses, while Gisburne leapt from his stallion, drawing his sword as he did so.

The abbot hastily shielded the newcomer. 'Wait, Gisburne!'

'But, my Lord!'

Hugo held up a commanding hand. 'No! I'll deal with this, you see to my brother.'

As Gisburne begrudgingly hauled his master from the thicket, Hugo reached a hand out to his unexpected visitor.

'Who are you?'

'Sanctuary!'

'Sanctuary?' The Abbot took in the man's mud-smeared, furrowed face, shock of grey hair and matted beard. Yet it was not this unkempt appearance that captured Hugo's attention, but the bright hazel eyes that shone out from underneath thick grey eyebrows. These were eyes that looked as if they should belong to a much younger man.

Opening his mouth to speak, the man in faded green, a ragged brown cowl draped over his shoulders, had no chance to utter another word, for Gisburne had returned. The Sheriff was by his side, gingerly pulling a collection of thorns from his sleeves.

'Hell's teeth, that hurt! Did you know you had thorn bushes so close to the abbey, Hugo?'

'So what if I have?'

'So what?' de Rainault winced, as he tugged a particularly sharp barb from his cheek. 'These thorns are like arrows. I could have been blinded—killed, even!'

'Oh do shut up, Robert.' Hugo shifted his attention to the limp figure before them, his tone calmer, 'You asked for sanctuary, stranger?'

Falling to his knees, his hands together as if in prayer, the supplicant opened his mouth to speak, but once again he had no chance to form his words, as the Sheriff had barged forwards.

'What is the meaning of this?'

'I am trying to find out, Robert.' Hugo sighed, reaching out an arm in welcome. 'Who are you?'

'A storyteller.'

Gisburne's expression pursed with distaste. 'A storyteller? Pah!'

The Sheriff, braver now Gisburne was brandishing a sword in the stranger's direction, peered imperiously down his nose. 'And what do you want?'

'Safety.' Lifting his clear eyes up to the Abbot, he added, 'And your counsel, my Lord.'

'My counsel?' Hugo raised his chin, his entire being projecting his authority in this place, and pushed the point of Gisburne's sword to one side. He approached the visitor, wrinkling his nose at the unwashed smell emanating from him, and gestured towards the abbey. 'Certainly, come this way.'

'Hugo! What are you doing?' The Sheriff demanded, jumping in front of his brother. 'You can't just invite him into the abbey; you have no idea who he is.'

'But I will find out. Go home to Nottingham, Robert, so I can carry out my Christian duty.'

'Christian duty? What's got into you Hugo?'

'My job.' Ignoring his brother's expression of horrified disdain, Hugo turned to address his visitor. 'What do they call you?'

'Many call me the Magic Man.'

Gisburne's eyes flashed with wary anger, as he repeated, incredulously, 'The Magic Man?'

'I do not believe in magic,' the Sheriff said as he backed away. 'I do believe you reek, though. When did you last wash?'

Taking heed of no one but the abbot, the Magic Man stretched out his hands. 'I make prophecies. Often, they come true... but lately... lately, they are all coming true—every part of them. I've begun to think... to believe that—'

De Rainault sneered, 'Hah! You can think, even though you can't wash? That's something, I suppose.'

'Robert!' The abbot growled before returning to the man knelt before him. 'Go on my friend; what is it you have started to believe?'

'I've begun to suspect, my Lord Abbot, that my visions are coming directly from God.'

CHAPTER TWO

Three days he'd been there, but still he could not get used to the cold. At least, not *this* level of cold. It bit cruelly at his fingers and toes; it gnawed at his cheeks.

'You should wear more layers. Sheepskin next to the skin, dyn drwg.'

He opened his mouth to curse Elis for his insolence, to tell him—yet again—that he should address him as "my Lord", but one look at the druid's scarred face and hard eyes made him bite his lip. He needed this man; he needed his knowledge, his abilities. Being called "dyn drwg"—whatever the hell it meant—was a small price to pay.

Finding this place—more stone-lined shack than a cave, more hovel than hermitage—had cost him dearly in both time and money. He just hoped that it would turn out to be worth his while.

He'd tried other ways to further his station, to attain the status and riches to which he knew he was entitled, but nothing had worked. He had even taken the bold step of petitioning the King to try and improve his lot. The memory of that still haunted him.

Pleading that it was only an accident of birth that saw him of lower rank than his far less capable older siblings, he had asked the King to assign him to a position that befitted his noble status and abilities.

A Sheriff, he shuddered. *And not JUST a mere Sheriff, forced to deal with lazy tax gatherers, criminals and the worthless masses, but a sheriff in Wales too!*

The insult had pierced his blackened soul like a spear.

Then, as he'd stormed through the castle, humiliation burning in his ears, an overheard conversation on the fringes of the stable block had stopped him in his tracks. Two soldiers had been discussing a group of men who knew how to harness magical powers. Druids who called themselves the Fferyllt.

Keeping out of sight of the gossiping guards, their Welsh accents jarringly out of place in the

English castle, he had listened as they'd spoken of a seemingly ageless man who had a knowledge few others possessed: a famed Fferyllt named Elis, who was fabled to keep himself hidden in the Welsh mountains.

Taking some time to think, he'd waited until the soldier's shift had ended, before cornering one of them.

Any member of the Fferyllt, he'd been told, was deliberately hard to find. There were rumours of the clan dying out, that one of only a few remained. And that one was Elis, a powerful druid who could influence the minds of others. Still dwelling deep within the Welsh mountains, his help could be purchased—for the right price—by those desperate enough to make the journey to find him.

From that moment, it had taken three months and two days to seek out his quarry. Two days ago he had found him, secreted in a nameless place in a godforsaken mountain range, in a land where the howl of the wind sounded like a raging pack of dogs, forever hungry.

A sheriff in Wales too! The irony had not been lost on him. *The King had the audacity to offer me a shrievalty here in this hell of mountains, forests, valleys and savages. Instead, this Godforsaken land will help me get my revenge, so I can become so much more than that.*

Elis had not been surprised to see him in the slightest when he'd stumbled through the goatskin that formed the door to his domain. Elis had even had food and drink waiting on his arrival, a fact that would have bothered him if he allowed himself to ponder upon it… so, he tried not to. Instead, he'd chosen to consider it a positive sign. If this druid was capable of knowing a petitioners' requirements before they reached his dwelling, then he could surely help him become the person he wished to be.

Anyway, every other avenue to power had escaped him. This was the best option for him now, even if it involved compromise.

A compromise that will go only as far as I want it to. When I'm done with Elis, I can simply walk away.

'Is that so, dyn drwg?'

Startled, he shook his head, to clear the internal monologue that Elis had somehow heard. 'Forgive me, old habits…'

'I'm sure.' The elderly druid didn't look up, but continued to mix a combination of ingredients into his wide-mouthed dish. 'You've been used to having what you want for as long as you want. You then discard things—including people—as if they are rubbish.'

'I—'

'I told you when you arrived that there is a price for my services. I trust you have not forgotten?'

'I have not forgotten.' Flicking his gaze around the room, he tried not to shiver. As he'd travelled from England to Wales, there had been many times in which he'd wondered if he'd been foolish in believing the druid could help him. But now, as he observed his quiet commanding certainty, he reassured himself. *He can help me*.

'You are right, dyn drwg. I *can* help you.'

The nobleman shuddered. 'I am not yet used to you being able to read the thoughts in my head.'

'It isn't just the thoughts in your head I see. Ambition seeps from you; it's an aura you carry—it burns red. You will carry that desire for power until the very end.'

His smile dropped. 'You see my ending?'

'I see everything…'

'Do I become all I deserve to be?'

'Oh yes, dyn drwg.'

He swallowed, 'Why do you call me *dyn drwg?*'

'It is your name here.'

'What does it mean?'

16

'It is simply who you are.' Elis threw some dust into the bowl. 'Tell me, what visions you have seen in the bowl so far?'

Frowning, he asked, 'Why must I repeat what has been seen?'

'I need to be sure you are paying attention.'

'You can read my thoughts, so surely you know what I've seen… and *you* saw it all too!'

Annoyingly calm, Elis kept his eyes on the sapphire liquid before him, his willow twig swirling though it in concentric circles. 'I know what you saw—but did you *understand* it?'

Taking a deep breath, knowing how foolish antagonising this being would be, he placed his hands on his belt. He missed the dagger and sword he usually kept there—Elis had insisted he relinquish them on his arrival.

Probably because I might have stabbed him in frustration by now if I still had them.

'That is correct. Now, tell me what you have seen.'

Blushing a deep crimson, embarrassed by how quickly he had, again, forgotten to guard his thoughts, he dug his fingernails into the palms of his hands, creating little crescents in his skin as he spoke. 'There was a man dressed in drab green clothing, with a brown cowl—too good a quality to be that of a peasant, yet nor was he a nobleman. He was running through the forest, talking to himself, claiming to see visions from God. He ran into a building I took to be an abbey, but I am less sure about that,'

'That is correct; it was an abbey. Good.' Elis dipped his hooded head. 'The man you saw is the one they called the Magic Man. He has always been able to gauge the future, but now he sees images that worry him. Images that come not from God, as he suspects, but from me.'

Regarding the druid with a mix of respect and dread, he asked, 'And how will that help me?'

'By watching the Magic Man, you will see the obstacles that prevent your rise to influence. Once you know who stands in your path, you can travel it with foreknowledge. In return for being shown who and what you need to see, you will kill him for me. That is the fee I charge for my aid. I trust it is acceptable?'

There was no hesitation in his answer. 'It is. The world is better off without mad men like him, but...'

'You desire to know why I long for his demise, dyn drwg?'

'Yes.'

'Because he is not just a man of magic. He is something far worse than that. That man—' Elis stabbed his twig back into the bowl, sending sparks flying to the ceiling, '—is a *storyteller.*'

CHAPTER THREE

Abbot Hugo flashed the Sheriff and Gisburne a warning glare as he knelt beside the bedraggled figure. 'God, you say?'

'Yes, my Lord Abbot. All my life I've been able to anticipate things that are going to happen, but I could always explain my thoughts. Logic and judgement were all that mattered. Such is my knowledge of the landscape, its people and the world in which we live, that intelligence and imagination were enough to help me forge a path to share wisdom. I could guide others with my foresight. But now, for the last month almost, every vision I've had has been *exact*, and everything I've seen has come to fruition.'

Hugo's eyes narrowed. 'You sound more like a

shaman than a prophet. A May Day charlatan, like Herne the Hunter.'

At the mention of Herne, the Magic Man leapt to his feet. A wild look came to his eyes and a strange expression fixed itself upon his face, as if he was no longer seeing any of them. 'The Lord of the Trees! You know of him?'

'Yes… I— *we* know about Herne.' Hugo retreated a few paces, suddenly desperate to get away from the glazed eyes as they seemed to morph from hazel to a vibrant sapphire. 'Are you… are you alright?'

The Magic Man clutched his hands together, holding them against his chest. With his spine bolt straight, he thrust his arms outwards and then to his sides, as if he was trying to encompass the whole world. 'I see them… they are in the forest… an ambush…'

'Ambush!' Gisburne raised his sword, only to have the abbot knock his arm down again.

'Listen to him, Gisburne!'

'But, my Lord Abbot—'

'He's no threat; look at his eyes. He's not even here—I mean, in his mind he's not here. He's having a premonition.'

All three noblemen, unconsciously shuffling closer together, observed the Magic Man. His eyes appeared to radiate a light outwards, as if they were taking on the sunset itself.

'Ambush… here at the abbey… mercenaries…'

This time it was the Abbot who spun around, as if expecting to see a hoard of fierce infiltrators dive out of Sherwood and appear behind them in a puff of smoke. 'Mercenaries?'

'Your food… hungry… it belongs to the people… so much food here… well stocked larder… they want it.'

'I *knew* it!' The Sheriff shouted, as the Magic Man reached up to the sky, shaking his thick head of hair as if trying to dispel the imagines that plagued his mind. 'Let's get inside, Hugo,' he urged, 'Gisburne and I will help lighten that larder of yours so—'

'No!'

The Magic Man's cry silenced Robert de Rainault mid-sentence. It left behind an icy silence, sending a creeping dread through the air which seeped into the walls of the abbey itself.

'A powerful man will be lost to you.'

'A powerful man?' The Sheriff exchanged a glance with his brother. 'Which one? There are so many. Unless you mean… could you mean *me?*'

The Magic Man's arms fell to his sides, his body crumpling into a heap. 'I'm so tired… so very tired.'

Rushing to his side, his dislike of the storyteller's bodily aroma dismissed in his desire to discover answers, the Sheriff asked, 'Do you know which powerful man you were talking about?'

'I fear I do not, my Lord.'

Intrigued, the Abbot nodded towards St Mary's. 'You may stay here. Supper and a place to sleep will be found for you.'

'Hugo! You can't mean to let this man inside the abbey? He speaks of magic, and yet you are a man of God!'

'Oh, so I *am* a Christian now am I, Robert? A few minutes ago you were accusing me of being far from that.' Turning his back on his brother, Abbot Hugo held an arm out to the Magic Man, who took it gratefully. 'This way. You're safe now.'

Once the Abbot was out of sight, Gisburne remounted his horse. 'Did you see the odd light that came to his eyes, my Lord?'

'I did, yes.' The Sheriff's own eyes narrowed. 'He was talking about Hood, wasn't he?'

'Perhaps, my Lord.'

'More than "perhaps", Gisburne! Who else would be so brazen as to plan to break into an abbey? Who else around here would bother to steal to help the poor?'

'He didn't say it was to help the poor—only that the food *belonged to the people.*'

'Don't split hairs, Gisburne!'

Ignoring his master, Sir Guy gestured towards the men-at-arms. 'I'm going to have a look around before we head to Nottingham. Guard the Sheriff.'

'No need,' de Rainault said as he peered up at the sky. Clouds had gathered, and nighttime was drawing in. 'I'm going inside. We will stay with the Abbot until morning. I want to make sure Hugo doesn't weaken and accidently become too nice to his guest.'

'As you wish, my Lord.' Gisburne placed a hand to his sword. 'I will join you soon.'

Elis smiled. 'Did you see the way his eyes morphed from brown to blue?' he asked.

'I wasn't looking at his face, I was—'

The druid's expression became pinched with disappointment as he turned to his visitor. 'If you do not pay attention, you will not get what you came here for.'

'Do not speak to me like—'

Cutting through the protest, Elis peered into the bowl. 'His eyes went blue because *I* was the one seeing through them. The blue matches that of the liquid in my bowl.'

A half-smile came to the visitor's face. 'You can influence his prophecies?'

'I can do many things, dyn drwg.' He tilted up his scrawny chin. '*Many* things.'

Thankful that he'd chosen his black stallion to ride to the abbey, knowing that it would blend into the shadows far better than his usual grey mount, Gisburne rode between the trees.

He wasn't sure why he didn't share the Sheriff's belief that the storyteller had been talking about Robin Hood. It was merely a feeling. A conviction, perhaps… that if Herne's Son *had* planned a visit to St Mary's, they'd have had no pre-warning from such a man. The outlaws would have simply acted, taken what they wanted, and gone again… and this so-called Magic Man would have let them, applauded the act even.

Listening hard as he rode, ducking under low-hanging branches, he paid attention to the fall of his horse's hooves, muffled by the leaf-covered ground. Gisburne hadn't gone far when the scent of a campfire reached his nostrils. Dismounting, he tethered the stallion to the nearest tree and crept forwards, a faint hum of conversation met his ears.

Hiding behind a wide oak trunk, Gisburne watched as a group of rough-looking men sat around the blaze in a small clearing. They were talking quietly as an ale pouch was shared between them, each taking a brief sip before passing it on.

Unsure if he was pleased to have been right or not—these were certainly not Hood's men—Gisburne took in their pinched faces. There was a hunger about their expressions, and not just for food. He'd seen men with such a look before—the storyteller was right about one thing; there were mercenaries in the forest.

Taking a step backwards, intending to alert the Abbot, the Sheriff, and their men at arms, Gisburne turned—and found himself face to face with a burly man sporting a big, black beard and very few teeth.

'Now what can we do for you, *Sir?*' He drawled, 'Or more to the point, what can *you* do for *us?*'

CHAPTER FOUR

Sparks flew straight upwards as a log was hurled onto the campfire. Seething with frustration and tired of arguing, Friar Tuck had run out of words.

'Tuck?' Marion looked at her friend in amazement. 'I've never seen you throw anything in your life!'

'He's thrown punches,' Little John winked playfully, but Tuck wasn't in the mood for being teased.

'I've had enough!'

'Enough of what?' Will rounded on the friar. 'You could have set the trees alight, chucking stuff at the fire like that! And then what? Not only would the villagers have next to nothing to eat, but they'd have no home either. And nor would we!'

'I know you're fed up, Tuck,' Robin of Loxley said as he sat down with a thump. 'We all are, but unless you can pray up some kind of miracle, then I don't know what we can do beyond breaking into the castle to steel the villagers' food back... and that's too dangerous.'

Marion was despondent. 'How can they be so cruel? The tithes the Church takes are already huge. The people only ever have just enough to get by— and what does the Sheriff do? He decides to top up his own larder by sending Gisburne to every village to raid it for food!'

'Calling it a "food tribute for the king",' Nasir snarled.

'Food tribute, my arse!' Will Scarlet cursed, joining Robin in the fire's deep orange glow. 'None of that grub will get further than Nottingham. I bet the king ain't got a clue what the Sheriff is up to.'

'Nothing unusual in that,' Little John agreed, stretching his arms upwards before clambering to his feet. 'Suppose I'd better go fishing again. You coming with me, Much?'

'Alright then.' Much jumped up, a crease forming on his young round face as he looked at Robin. 'Why would you want to break into the castle to get the food?'

Robin ruffled Much's hair. 'Because that's where the Sheriff's taken it.'

'No, it ain't; he's sent it to the abbey. Abbot Hugo's place.'

'What?' Robin looked at the others, each of whom wore an equally-surprised expression. 'How do you know that?'

'I 'eard it.'

Will frowned. 'When?'

'In the forest yesterday, when I was poaching for them rabbits.'

'Unsuccessfully,' Tuck complained, patting his grumbling belly.

'That ain't my fault, Tuck! I tried for ages, but I couldn't find any. Everyone's been poaching 'cause their food's been pinched.'

'It's alright Much,' Robin said calmly, a placating hand raised, 'no-one's blaming you. But tell us, what exactly did you hear?'

'Two guards patrolling. They was moaning about having to go to the abbey with the Sheriff and Gisburne and how they were risking their necks riding through the forest to guard food they'd never get to eat.'

Will sighed, 'That ain't them telling you that the food is at the abbey though, Much.'

'You interrupted me telling you what 'appened! I hadn't finished talking!'

Marion laid a hand on Much's arm. 'Go on.'

'They said they thought it was a pointless trip, as they didn't think Abbot Hugo would give them any of the food the Sheriff had had sent to his larders.'

A smile crossed Robin's face. 'Then, the answer to the village's problem is obvious. We mount a raid on the larders of the Abbey of St Mary's.'

Will Scarlet and Little John were already on their feet, but Tuck shook his head.

'No. We can't do that.'

'What?' John gaped in disbelief. 'Just now, you were so grumpy about the villagers' food being stolen that you nearly set Sherwood on fire. Now you won't go and fetch it so we can return it to its rightful owners.'

'We don't know for sure that it was the villagers' food that the Sheriff sent to Abbot Hugo—but, even if that's the case, my faith won't allow me to take part on a raid on an abbey. The food there isn't just for the Abbot; it's for the monks who live there and the local poor.'

'Of course it was the villagers' food, Tuck!' Will was stunned. 'We need that food. Our people need that food.'

'I will not raid a house of God. I just won't.' The friar crossed his arms over his ample belly, adding, 'And I don't want you to either.'

As one, the outlaws turned to Robin.

'Alright, Tuck.'

'What do you mean, "Alright Tuck"?' Will was flabbergasted. 'What's alright about this situation? The Sheriff stole the food an' gave it to his brother to stash. All we need to do is break in an' take it back.'

'I will go and speak to Herne.'

Tuck's eyebrows rose. 'I'm not sure that Herne's opinion will help this time, Robin.'

'Perhaps; perhaps not,' Robin answered as he pushed Albion into his belt and pulled his hood over his long dark hair, 'but I'm going to speak to him anyway. He might be able to suggest another way in which we can help the villagers that would mean we don't have to raid the abbey.'

As Robin disappeared through the trees, Will Scarlet muttered, 'Unless Herne can magically produce serval barns worth of food, then I ain't seeing how 'e'll be any use at all.'

It took all of Gisburne's willpower not to wrinkle his nose as the stench of the black-bearded mercenary's breath washed over him.

'What abbey?'

'St Mary's. It's just over there.' Waving a hand back the way he'd come, Gisburne tried not to wonder how two of the eight men who lounged around the fire had each lost an eye, but he couldn't help himself. *Did I give the order to have those eyes burnt out? Do they know who I am?*

The mercenary next to him turned to his companions. 'Didn't know we was so near holy ground. You lot seen any angels?'

As humourless laughter broke out around the camp fire, Gisburne exhaled. *They aren't from round here, which means they probably didn't lose their sight after poaching in Sherwood.*

'Abbeys normally contain a fat abbot and a load of monks. This one got a fat abbot in it?'

An image of Abbot Hugo's purple-robed frame flashed through Gisburne's mind. 'I wouldn't say "fat" but I'll admit, I wouldn't say that he goes hungry either.'

Greeting this comment with a howl of false laughter, the chief mercenary drew a knife from his belt. It was at Gisburne's throat in seconds.

'I tell you what... we ain't unreasonable men, so here's what I suggest 'appens next.'

No stranger to being threatened, Gisburne listened carefully.

'You are going to tell us how to find this abbey and it's larder. Well stocked, is it?'

'The Sheriff of Nottingham recently had it refilled.'

'Did he now?' The mercenary grinned at his men. 'And I'd wager that if the larder is full, then the wine cellar must be bulging.'

'I would imagine so.'

'Now isn't that handy.'

'Fortuitous, I'm sure.'

'Fort...' The mercenary fumbled over their visitor's fancy word. 'Whatever it is, it's where we're going. Our ale supplies are running low, and I'm dying for a drink.'

'You're always dying for a drink, Cedric,' one of the partly-blinded felons laughed.

'Yeah well, our life is thirsty work. And so is leading you lot.' Withdrawing the knife with such speed that Gisburne felt a brief draught as it moved away. 'Get up, you lot! We're going on a hunger strike,' Cedric ordered, failing to notice the double meaning of his words.

Gisburne scrambled to his feet, only to be knocked down again.

'Not you!'

'But, how will you find the abbey without me?'

'By following the directions you's about to give us. Now then,' Cedric pointed to one of his henchmen, 'Brandon, get one of the horses tied to the wagon while I speak to our guest.'

Gisburne tensed further. 'I don't know what else I can tell you.'

'Well, that's a strange thing because I know exactly what you can tell me: for a start, who you are, what exactly you're worth, and how you know that it was the Sheriff himself who had the abbey's larder stocked!'

CHAPTER FIVE

Robin slowed his pace as he approached the mouth of the cave, before calling out, 'Herne.'

'I was expecting you.'

'I've come to tell you that the peoples' food is being stored at the abbey, but…'

'But it seems that there is one who stops you; one whose gift is equal to mine… a man of magic who foresees all.'

Robin was puzzled. 'I was talking about Tuck. He doesn't want us to raid the abbey—but I don't think he foresees all.'

Herne stretched his arms out to either side as he peered into a horizon far beyond Robin and Sherwood. 'Cave and stone, forest and mountain, collude and collide with avarice. An ancient power has found human greed and seized control of another. You must fight one who isn't there.'

'*One who isn't there?*' Robin replied, confused. 'I only came to find out if you thought it was appropriate for us to retrieve the supplies the Sheriff stole now that they're being kept on holy ground. The people are hungry, and—'

'I am not here to tell you what is right and what is wrong.'

Robin shook his head. 'If we take back the food, then Tuck will be upset. But, if we don't, the people of the forest will begin to starve.'

Herne lowered his antlered head, his eyes boring into those of his chosen son. 'I have spoken. He is in the stone and hides within another's words… you *must* listen.'

'I listen Herne, but I know not what I ought to be doing,' Robin implored, hoping for some clearer guidance.

There was a brief silence, as Robin waited in thought whilst Herne stood stoically in the cave's entrance. Then, turning on his heels, Robin headed back the way he'd come, mind made up. 'I'll go to the abbey,' he announced.

'Be careful, my son. A power is there… a power from which I cannot protect you.'

But Herne's warning fell on deaf ears, for the Hooded Man had already left.

Gisburne watched in silence as the mercenaries made their plans. As much as he'd have liked to tell them exactly what he thought of them, he hadn't survived working for the Abbot and then the Sheriff without knowing that sometimes it was better to hold his tongue.

Brandon, the mercenary who had been sent to fetch his steed, had already been dispatched to the abbey, and Gisburne could tell it wouldn't be long before the others followed, now they were in the process of tethering a horse to a wagon, ready to fill it with any food and alcohol they could find. The only matter still to be decided was which of them would stay behind to guard him, their prisoner.

'Will you *stop* pacing!' The Sheriff of Nottingham pleaded, before taking a brief pause from berating his brother to take another swig of claret. 'What is the matter with you, Hugo?'

'I told you Robert, I want to know more about this Magic Man.'

'What for? He's clearly insane, deluded or both. Let me take him to Nottingham and throw him in the dungeon.'

'He has asked me for sanctuary; I have a duty to—'

'You have a duty to *me*, the Sheriff of Nottingham!'

Hugo sat down opposite his brother. 'I'm going to see if he's alright.'

'What? *Why?*' The Sheriff was incredulous.

'He's had some time alone in the chapel to calm himself. Now I want to talk to him about these visions he claims he's been having.'

'It's pointless, Hugo; he's deranged!'

'Deranged, is he? Then why did you send men to guard the larders as soon as we'd heard him speak of mercenaries in the forest?'

'Nothing more than common sense. If some local idiot has worked out that *this* is where we're storing the additional food tithe, then Hood and his men may have worked it out too. They might try and get it back.'

'Gisburne didn't think the Magic Man's vision referred to Robin Hood.'

'Gisburne is a dolt.' The Sheriff stood with a sigh, 'But if you want to play along with whatever game this soothsayer creature is playing, then you carry on. I'm going to bed.'

'What about Gisburne? Are you not worried that he hasn't yet returned?'

'He can look after himself.'

'Can he?' The abbot was surprised by the notion.

'Well… sometimes he can,' the Sheriff shrugged. 'And anyway, it was his idea to wander off into the forest at night, so he only has himself to blame if he's blundered into trouble.'

'You talk as though he's expendable.'

'Oh come on, Hugo! You know how hopeless Gisburne is! We only keep him around because we enjoy laughing at his mistakes so much. Plus, he's a soldier… and soldiers occasionally get killed. It's a fact of life.'

'For God's sake, Robert! Sometimes you really are—'

The Abbot broke off as the sound of running sandals heading towards them echoed across the stone floor.

'Brother porter?'

Wheezing slightly, a flustered monk stumbled to a halt. 'My Lord Abbot, forgive me, I... a man... he... I—'

'What he's *trying* to say,' a figure said as he emerged from the shadows, 'is that he has a message for you.'

The colour drained from Hugo's face as he crossed himself. 'How in God's name did you get in here without us hearing?'

'I'm good at moving without a sound; you might think of it as a... God-given gift.' Brandon flashed a short-bladed sword through the air with one hand, while the other gripped hold of the quivering porter's shoulder. 'Now, what was it I heard you saying about Sir Guy of Gisburne being expendable?'

The Sheriff's eyes widened. 'How long have you been in here?'

'Long enough.'

The porter blustered, 'I'm sorry, my Lords, I don't know how he got past me, and then—' He broke off instantly as the tip of Brandon's blade poked meaningfully against his back.

'I don't believe you think your colleague *quite* as expendable as you claim. In fact, I believe you would want to exchange Sir Guy's life for a wagon's worth of food and wine, wouldn't you?'

The Abbot swung around to look at his brother as he muttered, 'Mercenaries in the forest!'

Brandon shook his head. 'We prefer to see ourselves as wanderers, doing our best to survive in today's somewhat trying circumstances.'

'I bet you do.' The Abbot put his hands on his hips. 'How dare you wave about a sword on this holy ground!'

'Sometimes we need to make a point, Abbot. A sharp one.' With a mock bow, Brandon lowered his sword. 'Our wagon awaits by the gatehouse. Once you have sent your monks to fill it with supplies, we will let your Gisburne go.'

'We don't care about Gisburne,' the Sheriff grunted.

'Do you care about this monk?' The mercenary placed a huge hand against the frightened porter's throat.

'Let him go,' Hugo shouted, 'you can have your wagon's worth of food! Now get out of here while I arrange things.'

'Certainly, my Lord Abbot,' Brandon smirked, 'though Brother porter here will be coming with me. You have one hour. After that, if you haven't done as I ask, you can say goodbye to your monk and Sir Guy.'

Neither of the de Rainault brothers spoke as the mercenary left, his boots making no sound as he dragged the frightened monk after him.

Only when they were sure that the invader had gone, did the Abbot move purposefully towards the door.

'Where are you going, Hugo? Surely you aren't going to let them have our food?'

'I'm going to the chapel, Robert.'

'To pray?'

'No, brother. To talk to the Magic Man.'

'Whatever for?'

'Don't you pay attention to anything?' The abbot rolled his eyes. 'I'm going to the chapel to talk to our guest because—in case you haven't noticed—his prophecy has come true!'

CHAPTER SIX

The acrid stench coming from the smog that hung over the bowl on the fire was turning his stomach. Fighting the urge to retch, he wiped his eyes with the back of a palm; despite standing as far as he could from the controlled blaze, they were watering fast, giving the illusion of tears as the multi-coloured smoke that rose from the fire stung his face. They were not tears though; even as a child he'd never wasted time crying.

'Dyn drwg, how can you hope to learn from me if you refuse to observe my actions closely?' Elis the druid beckoned to his client with an urgent hand. 'Come here, now!'

Inwardly smarting from the tone of the imperial command from someone of inferior standing to himself, he approached, nonetheless. Elis was tapping his willow stick against the side of the bowl. The rhythm was off kilter—each time he felt that a melody had begun, the tempo changed, leaving his ears feeling jarred, as if robbed of the sound his brain had predicted would come next.

The druid's long, thin, index finger jabbed at the haze rising over the bowl.

'Watch... learn... *understand...*'

Trying to close his nostrils to the smell, he peered into the bowl. A moment later he blinked, not against the smoky fumes, but at the picture which appeared in its blue midst.

It showed a man, young with long brown hair; there was a longbow hooked over his shoulder. He was talking to a monk as they walked through the forest. No, it wasn't a monk, it was a friar... a fat friar...

'I know you aren't happy about this Tuck, but we have no choice. The people need their food. We need them to get their food, as they often feed us in exchange for helping them. How long can we keep striving for what's right if even our stomachs are empty and we become too weak to fight?'

Unhappy, caught between his loyalty to his faith and his desire to help his friends, Tuck stopped moving. 'I can't, Robin... I just can't break into an abbey.'

'But Tuck, this ain't any old abbey. That pathetic excuse of an abbot, Hugo, lives here. And—' Will's exasperation was interrupted by Tuck's shout.

'It's still holy ground, Scarlet.'

Raising his hand, Robin stepped in before a full-blown row cost them precious time. 'Look, we are already nearing the crossroads that will take us in the direction of St Mary's. Could you come with us and act as lookout instead, Tuck?'

'Yes... yes, I think I can do that.'

'Alright then, let's go.'

Leading the way, Marion waved to the left as they reached the pathway that ran from the main body of Sherwood towards St Mary's. It had been just over a year since she'd last visited the abbey, a period that already meant that the past felt like another life. Her months as Abbot Hugo's ward might have been the most miserable time of her life, but it had given her an excellent knowledge of the layout of both Nottingham Castle and the abbey.

With Nasir on her heels, Robin behind her, and John, Will and Much keeping watch to the left and right, Marion moved swiftly. Half a mile later, she held up a hand to indicate they should come to a stop.

'Who are they?'

'Part of the game—the long game.' Elis scrutinised his visitor. '*Your* game. Pay attention, dyn drwg. The picture is about to change.'

Intrigued now, he moved closer to the bowl. A new scene emerged through the now pale blue smoke.

'Another cleric… an abbot… and…' He looked up sharply at Elis as he saw a new figure appear within the vision. 'That's him isn't it?'

'Oh yes. That's him. That's the storyteller. The Magic Man.'

Abbot Hugo found his visitor on the floor of the chapel. Face down, he was lying with his arms outstretched; his body forming the shape of a cross, as if he were offering up penance.

A jumble of words escaped from the man's mouth—whispered, muddled and desperate, 'The mountains... I see him... blue fog... eyes so dark... food... and he comes. They come; they come now... and there are others...' The Magic Man's head rocked from side to side on the hard stone ground. 'The prophecy... it is clouded. He seeks to block... to mould.' Sweat pooled in the small of his back as he murmured, 'Some to help, some to hinder... the mountains...'

'Hinder the mountains? I told you, Hugo; he's mad.' Mumbling about the interloper, the Sheriff moved further into the chapel.

Ignoring his brother, Abbot Hugo crouched next to the Magic Man. 'A mercenary has broken into the abbey. You were right. I have instructed some of my monks to give him food from the larders. If I don't, he'll kill two men.'

'Stories...' the Magic Man announced, now curled up into a ball on the floor. 'They are stories... we all become stories in the end.'

'Since when did mercenaries ever "become

47

stories"? He's spouting nonsense. This is a waste of time, Hugo. We should be hunting down these felons.'

'Oh, really? You're volunteering to go out there yourself are you, Robert?'

The Magic Man sat upwards; his hazel eyes appeared to radiate warmth. 'They are here. Now. He sent them.'

'We know they are here! We told you that!' The Sheriff had had enough. 'Hugo, we have work to do!'

The Abbot remained on his knees. 'Who? Who sent them? Who is this "he"?'

As his eyes rolled back in his head, the Magic Man whispered, 'Two of them… two messengers… one is stronger… blots the other… but he fights like I fight—with words. Mountains… cold… and… blood on bread…'

'Mountains?' Hugo's already worried expression paled. He crossed himself again. 'Did you say "blood on bread"?'

'Two of them… don't chase the wrong spirit…'

'Spirit?'

'They both have it… so much spirit…'

Abruptly, the Magic Man stilled; his body went limp, his eyes closing. For a horrifying second,

Hugo thought he'd died, but the rise and fall of his chest told him that their visitor had merely passed out.

Climbing to his feet, his knees cracking slightly from the cold of the stone chapel, Hugo mumbled to himself. 'Two of them... two of whom? Two mercenaries? Two spirits?' A chill that had nothing to do with the temperature of the room trickled through his purple-robed body. 'Herne and Robin Hood? But I wouldn't have said that Hood was a spirit... so who could the other one be?'

With these thoughts swirling in his head, Abbot Hugo strode from the chapel in pursuit of his brother.

'The man who stormed out of the chapel; who is he?'

'Robert de Rainault, the Sheriff of Nottingham.'

'Hah,' he sneered. 'The King offered me a shrievalty. *Me!*'

Elis cracked his willow twig against the side of the bowl as he chastised, 'Dyn drwg, you have not been paying attention.'

A hot sweat broke out on the nobleman's chest

as he peered into the vessel. The pictures had disappeared, the smoke nothing more than an impenetrable fog. Whatever vision that might have presented itself was now gone.

Hah! he thought. *Why did I think this would work? I've come all this way… and for what? To see images of people hundreds of miles away that have nothing to do with me!*

'They are everything to do with you! They are your future!' Elis threw down the willow; his eyes were as hard as flint. 'You have broken the cycle; you could have seen, but now…'

But his visitor was too steeped in his own thoughts to pay attention to the druid's anger.

I am worth so much more than the role of sheriff! And to be given a post in Wales rather than England? An insult too f—

'Dyn drwg, your thoughts offend me. Leave. Now.'

Marion spoke quickly and quietly. 'The back way into the larder is through the walled garden. There's a narrow entrance into the garden down there.'

Nasir led the group towards the indicated green door set in the long stone-built wall that towered high above them.

'Once we are through here, we must stick to the shadows around the right edge of the garden. But we will need to break cover eventually to get to the larder door. It's kept locked.'

'Aye, lass,' Little John said, patting his quarterstaff, 'but I've never met a barn lock *this* can't knock from its fixings.'

'How about guards?' Will asked.

'There never used to be any,' Marion replied, scooping her hair over her shoulders, 'though it's been a while since I was here.'

Robin felt an echo of Herne's warning at the back of his mind. 'The Sheriff may well have put some guards there now, to protect his tithe.'

'Makes sense,' Will agreed, drawing his sword from his belt in readiness.

'It's always quite dark inside,' Marion warned. 'The food will be stacked on the left as we go in. The wine and ale is kept in the cellar below.'

'Much, Will, Nasir, Marion: you concentrate on filling these with food.' Robin handed out sacks from a roll he'd been carrying under his arm. 'John and I will get some ale pouches.'

'And maybe some wine for you, Tuck?' Marion asked, smiling at the cleric.

'Thank you, Little Flower. But don't take anything for me. If you must do this, then food is the priority. Get in and get out, so we can get back to Sherwood before a single monk has the chance to utter a prayer against us.'

'Stay safe, Tuck,' Robin said, patting his friend's shoulder. 'If you see anything, make the call of an owl.'

Much's earnest face turned to Robin as he asked, 'It's getting dark already, what if a *real* owl calls?'

Having no answer to that, Robin opened the door, smiled and crept into the garden.

CHAPTER SEVEN

Gisburne watched his lone guard carefully.

Having been left to watch their captive, the solo mercenary quickly finished off the little remaining ale and, slumped by the fire, soon slipped into a light doze.

As soon as he's properly asleep…

The ropes that had bound Gisburne's wrists had come loose with an ease that would have embarrassed the mercenaries' leader. Sir Guy almost wished he could stay around to gloat about the ease of his escape, but he had more immediate plans.

Rising quietly to his feet, he took a step backwards, his eyes fixed upon the snoozing man.

I would be a better leader of these men than the sorry excuse currently in charge.

He travelled on tiptoed feet, avoiding every leaf and twig. Only when Gisburne was sure he was well out of earshot of the camp did he exhale in relief.

Making his way to where he hoped his stallion would still be waiting for him, he thought fast.

Do I go to the castle, the abbey… or do I leave and find a place where I'm actually appreciated?

If he'd thought it had been cold in the mountains when he'd first arrived here, that was nothing to the crippling chill he was experiencing now. The wind froze his bones as it screamed and howled, lashing at him from every direction.

Winter was some months away, yet he could see snow already capping the summits that rose around him, jagged and menacing in the dark.

He knew that if he stayed here, he'd never make it through the night, but if he went back…

If you come back, dyn drwg, you will vow to obey without question… to do as I command while you are in the realm of the Fferyllt.

Rotating fast on the spot, he expected to see Elis behind him, but there was no one there.

I speak to the inside of your mind from my cave. Follow my voice if you want to live, if you truly want to see where my skills can take you. But first... first you must agree to my terms.

'You speak to me as if I'm a servant! Do you not know who I am?'

You are dyn drwg, and without me you are nothing. And without my food and my fireside, right now you walk the road to becoming a dead man.

There were no guards patrolling the rear of the larder.

Just as Marion had predicted, the wooden door was fixed shut with a padlock. Looking around, double-checking they were alone, Robin nodded at John, who smacked his staff against the door, instantly rendering the lock pointless.

Not waiting to see if the thud of the staff or fall of the lock onto the grass had alerted the monks to their presence, Robin threw open the door.

Much dived inside, his sack already half open to fill with the food he'd been daydreaming about eating all the way there.

A second later and all the outlaws were now stood within the dark space.

A second after *that*, the door slammed shut behind them and a laughing figure lit a candle.

'Robin of Loxley… how *nice* to see you again,' the Sheriff of Nottingham beamed, his smile all the more sinister in the guttering candlelight, 'and how thoughtful of you to bring your fellow outlaws with you.'

The Magic Man sat up slowly, massaging his forehead.

He ached not with cold nor fatigue; he ached with the effort of blocking *him* out.

Until he'd swooned, he hadn't been sure who it was who'd managed to break into his thoughts— although he'd certainly had his suspicions. But now, thanks to his latest vision, he *knew*, for he had seen the mountains and felt the cold.

His concentration must have slipped, otherwise he'd never have allowed me to see where he is.

'My Lord God, I know now that it is not you who sends these messages,' the Magic Man declared.

Crawling on all fours towards the chapel's altar, he clasped his hands together and prayed, 'I beseech thee: give me the wisdom and strength to fend off this evil; show me what I must do.'

An image of the face he'd seen in his mind just before he'd fallen into a faint reared up again in his mind, and he shivered.

'Fferyllt.'

Tuck shifted anxiously from foot to foot. He'd known that filling the sacks would take a while, but his friends had been gone for far longer than he'd expected.

Guilt nudged at him. *I should have gone with them.*

Peering upwards, Tuck could see the top of the abbey's roof through the trees, its beautifully crafted stonework outlined in the starlight.

No... I can't. I couldn't steal from holy ground, not even for Robin.

Wrapping his cloak around him, he shuffled nearer to the narrow doorway that led into the garden and listened. The faint rustle of the trees dimmed, and a sense of foreboding trickled through his body.

'Brother Tuck... can you hear me? I see you...'

Spinning round, Tuck drew his sword... but there was no one there.

'Hello?' Tuck whispered, as a chill ran through him.

'Find me... find me...'

As the voice faded, Tuck took in some steadying breaths and tried to think. He was sure it hadn't been Herne.

'Someone needs my help,' Tuck whispered to himself. Wiping his palms down his front, he kept hold of the sword and edged through the doorway and into the garden, unused to the level of fear that stirred in his stomach.

He could just make out the entrance to the larder. Though it was ajar, he could see no shadows moving inside, nor could he hear any sound. In fact, there was nothing but a sense of absence—that no one was in there at all.

Something's wrong, Tuck thought. Feeling vulnerable and alone, the friar snuck closer, his bulk almost filling the doorway as he realised that he wasn't only feeling his own fear, but experiencing someone else's as well.

'I'm in the chapel... please come... your friends need us both.'

Tuck gripped the handle of his sword even tighter and, pushing his shoulders back, strode purposefully into the walled garden.

Robert de Rainault was enjoying himself.

Ever since Robin of Loxley had taken to the forest and gathered a motley band of followers around him, the Sheriff had dreamt of this. Countless times he'd pictured having them under his control—captured, afraid—and wondered how he'd have them killed. Now he'd done it!

Where is Gisburne? He'd like this... although... a loud, hard chuckle left his throat... *he'd hate that I have imprisoned Herne's Son without any help from him at all. He'll be furious when he finds out.*

With a gesture to the guard on the door, the Sheriff glided into the long, thin dark room. 'I trust you are uncomfortable, Wolfshead.'

'I'm fine, thank you, Sheriff.' Sat on a wooden stool, arms tied behind him and ankles fixed to the front two legs of his hard seat, Robin surveyed the scene. 'The abbey's larder is well stocked,' he said. 'You didn't inflict the new food tithe on Abbot Hugo, then?'

Taking no notice of the insinuation, the Sheriff looked from one outlaw to the next. 'Enjoy your night here; it will be your last.'

Will Scarlet opened his mouth to protest, but Robin shot him a warning glance before saying, 'If you plan to execute us, Sheriff, you'll have to take us away from here.'

Marion found her voice, 'You cannot murder us on holy ground. The Pope has rules.'

'I don't *care* what the Pope…'

'Your *brother* would care, though,' Robin stated, keeping his voice level.

The Sheriff held the outlaw's gaze before turning away. He had almost reached the door when he realised someone was missing.

'The friar… where is he?'

'Back at the camp.'

'Hmm…' de Rainault said, eyes narrowing. 'Why do I find that hard to believe?'

'I've no idea, Sheriff. A suspicious nature, perhaps?' Robin's expression gave nothing away.

De Rainault marched to the door, annoyed that this moment—which should have felt like a victory—seemed inexplicably sour. *I've captured all but one of them; they'll be dead in two days time... and yet still they mock me...*

Once he had returned to the abbey's refectory, de Rainault called to the nearest guard, 'Friar Tuck isn't with them. They *say* he remained in Sherwood, but I'm not so sure.'

'I understand, my Lord, I'll get a search of the area underway.'

'Good.' The Sheriff nodded with satisfaction before adding, 'But only *after* you have doubled the guard on this door.'

'I would, my Lord, but there's a limited number of soldiers here, and—'

'Do it!' The Sheriff's face shone bright and red as a beetroot.

'Yes, my Lord.'

Tuck's progress was halted by the arrival of three guards he'd seen emerge from the larder door.

Slinking into the shadows, he thought fast. *If they've caught the others, then they'll likely be looking for me.*

Watching as two of the soldiers walked across the garden, closing in on where he was hiding, Tuck considered his options.

I knew it was a mistake to invade an abbey. If only Robin had listened to me! But there's someone else who needs our help... my help...

Abandoning any thought of getting into the abbey unnoticed, he brushed down his robes, and walked straight into the open heart of the garden.

'Guards! I *must* speak to Abbot Hugo. It's urgent!'

CHAPTER EIGHT

'And why should I believe you?'

Tuck folded his hands over his ample stomach as he sat opposite the Abbot of St Mary's in his private office. 'There is no reason why you should, my Lord,' he agreed, before continuing, 'however, despite all you know of my life in recent times, you *also* know that my first loyalty has always been to Our Lord God.'

'Which is why, you claim, you did not join your fellow felons in trying to steal from an abbey. *This* abbey!'

'I can only apologise, my Lord Abbot, for the fact that I could not dissuade Robin from raiding the abbey's larder.' He clenched his hands together. 'The welfare of the people will always come first for him. I cannot criticise him for that... but in this case, I could not support him either.'

'And yet you were found outside the garden, acting as his lookout.'

'*No*, my Lord.' Tuck sent a private apology up to heaven for the lie he was about to tell, 'I was troubled by my conscience, and so followed them here to try—once more—to dissuade them from what they were about to do.'

Abbot Hugo reached for a nearby jug, and filled a cup with wine. 'What do you want, Brother Tuck?'

'My friends did not return, so I assume you have them under lock and key. I'd like you to let them go.'

'I'm sure you would.'

Tuck gave a heavy sigh, leaning forwards as he spoke, 'I have decided to leave them. Leave Sherwood. Go back into the cloister—as a monk this time, not a friar.'

Hugo's arm paused in the act of lifting his cup to his lips. 'I beg your pardon?'

'You heard me.' Tuck felt his heart race in his chest, as a sense of sadness engulfed him. 'Prior to my departure from here, I am asking for you to release my friends—but it's more than that. I'm asking you to help the *people*, by freeing Robin and the others. Your people—the very people who tend the land for this abbey and for your brother in Nottingham—*need* Robin Hood to care for them when you cannot. You do not always know what is right for them. Sometimes, in fact, you do... then ignore your instincts in favour of your own comforts.'

'You speak with arrogance, Tuck. What makes you so sure that *you* know what is right for the people and *I* don't?'

'I live amongst them, my Lord Abbot. I have no roof over my head and I don't always know where the next meal is coming from. You have a warm bed, a chamber to sleep in, servants and cooks...' Tuck held his open palms out before him, 'It is as simple as that.'

Hugo got to his feet. 'There is nothing simple about this at all. You cannot imagine the pressures I face from the Crown, the Pope, the—'

Tuck broke through the abbot's protests, 'I have *some* idea. I lived in Nottingham Castle, remember? I saw how you and the Sheriff treat people... and how you cope with the demands of your position. It is something you have always taken rather a—shall we say—*convenient* approach too.'

'How dare you!'

'I dare, because I must. Because something here now feels wrong... although I know neither what nor why. But I would like to find out. Perhaps we could go to the chapel.'

'The chapel?'

'Yes, my Lord. I find I crave guidance. Can you think of a better place than before an altar to seek such a thing?'

When Hugo didn't reply, Tuck was convinced that whoever it was who'd urged him to come to the chapel, Hugo knew about them. *'Is* there something wrong, my Lord Abbot?' he asked.

Knocking back his wine in one huge gulp, Hugo slammed the cup onto the table and headed for the door. 'Come with me, Brother Tuck.'

As soon as he saw the grey-haired man, the friar knew that this was the person who'd invaded his thoughts. A sense of familiarity he did not understand flowed through him.

Hugo whispered, 'Brother Tuck, are you alright?'

'I— I feel as though I know this man, and yet I've never seen him before in my life.'

The Abbot gave him a sharp look. 'I remind you that we are in the chapel. Here we are as close to God as it gets. You will not lie to me.'

'I wouldn't... and I couldn't.'

Hugo searched the outlaw's face for signs of deception, but found none. 'I believe you,' he admitted.

'You are right to do so,' Tuck said, stepping forwards. 'Who is he?'

'He calls himself the Magic Man... and a storyteller.' The abbot shook his head. 'I can't believe I'm even saying this—let alone to you—but he says he sees things... that he receives messages from God.'

Tuck's eyebrows rose. 'That is some claim.'

'Yes, which is why I wondered... could he be a messenger from Herne?'

This time Tuck was the one wearing open disbelief on his face. 'You believe in Herne, Abbot Hugo?'

'Let us just say that I've been in and around the forest for long enough to know how influential belief can be.'

Wondering if he'd misjudged the Abbot, Tuck approached the figure kneeling by the altar and asked, 'Did you call to me?'

'I did,' the man in green and brown confirmed, though he did not move; his hands remained folded together before him, his eyes screwed up in concentration.

'Who are you?'

'The Magic Man.'

'What sort of magic?' Tuck tilted his head to one side. 'There are so many kinds... good, evil, self-attaining—'

'Story magic.' The man opened his eyes. 'I know your story, Friar Tuck... I see the words. I read events, I see what has been... and I predict how things will play out, how the stories will unfold.'

'Stories?'

The Magic Man screwed his eyes tightly shut as he breathed, *'You're welcome, Little Flower.'*

Tuck gasped. 'Marion! Is she alright... is Marion..?'

Turning to face Tuck, the storyteller nodded. 'She will always be your Little Flower.'

Hugo placed a hand on a confused Tuck's shoulder. 'Robert thinks he's mad—deluded.'

'But you aren't so sure?'

'I am not. How did he know your name for Marion?'

Tuck shrugged. 'Both you and the Sheriff knew

from when I lived in the castle; perhaps he heard tales of my time as the Sheriff's chaplain?'

Hugo's expression made it clear he was not convinced by the friar's theory. 'He arrived asking for sanctuary, and he's caused no trouble since. He even warned us about the food being stolen.'

Tuck's eyes narrowed. 'He told you that Robin was coming?'

'He told us that mercenaries were coming—and he was right.'

'We are not mercenaries. They take for themselves. We do not.'

'I know, Tuck.' Hugo had neither the time nor the inclination to debate the matter. 'Initially, it seemed obvious to my brother that it must be Hood of whom this man spoke. But then a genuine mercenary broke into the abbey, demanding food and drink.'

'But then Robin arrived too...'

'...and walked right into the trap we'd set for this other felon's men.'

'I see.'

'Tuck, what if...' the abbot lowered his voice, '...this Magic Man really is a conduit for God?'

'Then we should treat him with the utmost respect.'

The Abbot moved further from the altar. 'But he's a vagrant. I mean… just look at him. He wears peasants breeches and tunic, and a hood, and—'

'And Jesus was a lowly carpenter,' Tuck hissed angrily. 'You have been spending too much time with your brother, Abbot. You forget your vocation.'

Stung—though unable to argue—Hugo strode back to face the Magic Man, his expression purposeful. 'Why have you really come here, Storyteller?'

When the Magic Man spoke, he did not answer the question. Instead he issued a statement of fact, 'The friar is here to rescue his fellow outlaws.'

Two points of colour warmed Tuck's cheeks as he stared in horror at the praying man. 'I came to help you! You called me.'

'And you came. But you intend to try and free your friends, do you not?'

'I knew it!' The door to the chapel clicked shut behind the Sheriff of Nottingham as he arrived. 'I told you, Hugo. When will you learn to listen to me?'

Cursing himself for not listening out for trouble, Friar Tuck froze as he saw the triumphant grin on the Sheriff's face. 'My Lord, I…'

'Save it! You can bleat to the executioner alongside Loxley, the Lady Marion and the others.

70

Guards!' On his bellow, two soldiers burst into the chapel.

'Robert! This is hallowed ground!'

'This is no time for your false piety, Hugo!' The Sheriff pointed towards Tuck, demanding, 'Take him to the larder with the others.'

As the guards grabbed hold of him, Tuck kept his focus on the kneeling man. 'You called to me for help!'

'Yes. And you *will* help. The stories say that—'

'Hah! It is exactly as I thought,' the Sheriff interrupted. 'This man is no more talking to God than I am. This sounds like the sort of nonsense that Herne is said to spout!'

Hugo's expression darkened. 'I think perhaps you are right, brother. Get this outlaw out of here!'

'But my Lord Abbot! I—'

'Not one more word, Tuck. Not *one,*' the Sheriff yelled, his temper seemingly exaggerated by the echoes of the stone. 'Hugo, have this not-so-magic conman locked up with them as well. Then, for goodness sake, let us get some sleep. Tomorrow, we have prisoners to transfer safely to Nottingham.' A wide, cruel smile crossed his lips, 'Although that will be much easier than it used to be, as Robin Hood is hardly going to rescue *himself,* is he?'

CHAPTER NINE

Hate radiated from him. Hate for the man he was relying on to help him. Hate for himself for seeking the assistance of someone else in the first place. Hate for his mother for not giving birth to him first. Hate for his brothers for coming before him. And hate for a system that placed him in a hierarchy that he could not control.

Most of all however, he hated the humiliation he felt as the wind, rain and cold forced him to re-enter Elis's domain.

'Approach, dyn drwg.'

Grateful the druid commented on neither his truculent absence nor his inevitable return, he obeyed, and waited by the fire that—this time— shone with a sickly turquoise flame. When the hush between himself and Elis became uncomfortably long, however, he snapped, 'And?'

'Will you obey me from now on?'

'Yes,' he grunted, 'though I would like to know why you want me to kill this... Magic Man.'

Elis's eyebrows rose. 'Would you? And when did you become so worried about having a reason to dispatch someone to Hell?'

'We have to get out of here.'

'Of course we do, Much,' Will growled, 'but that ain't so easy. These ropes are knotted fast.'

Robin chafed again at his own bound wrists. 'They aren't taking any chances. They've learnt from our previous escapes.'

'And so have I,' Marion whispered as she wriggled her arms behind her until, suddenly, they were free. 'There!'

'Oh well done lass,' John beamed.

'Small wrists,' Marion laughed, and was about to lean forward to free her ankles from the front legs of the chair upon which she's been restrained when Nasir made an urgent shushing noise.

At once the male outlaws froze, while Marion thrust her arms behind her as the outer door to the larder creaked open.

Not one of them spoke as they watched Tuck being ushered in to join them, and how he was thrust down onto another seat before being tied up.

A moment later, the sound of flailing limbs met their ears and another prisoner was dragged in. This time, the soldiers escorting their captive were red in the face with effort as a slim man with grey hair and bright hazel eyes was thrown to the floor.

'Leave him be,' Tuck shouted as one of the guards kicked the Magic Man in the stomach, sending him sprawling.

'Be quiet,' one of the guards ordered as he tethered the Magic Man's arms. 'You there, secure his ankles.'

As a second guard fastened a slim line of rope around this latest prisoner's legs, Tuck chastised them, 'You are making a terrible mistake. This man is channelling God Himself!'

'You speak blasphemy, Friar!'

'Do I?' Tuck rounded on the guard, all the time aware of the heat of his friends' gaze on his back. 'Or do you endanger your immortal soul by hauling him here?'

Muttering to themselves, the guards left quickly. There was a cry of "Make sure you guard this place well" shouted to a colleague as the door was banged shut and a hush descended on the inside of the larder.

A warning glance from Robin was enough to tell the other outlaws not to speak yet. It wasn't until a frustrating ten minutes or more had passed that Robin looked towards his wife.

'Marion, untie us please.' Watching the man on the floor, he asked Tuck, 'What's going on?'

'That man... he has magic. But more than that, he *sees* things.'

'Oh no, not another one,' Will groaned. 'Herne is bad enough by himself!'

'Herne has guided us and saved our lives many times,' Robin reminded his friend, with rather more of an edge to his voice than he had intended.

Not wanting them to become sidetracked, Tuck spoke fast as Robin—now free—helped Marion rescue the others. 'Abbot Hugo is afraid of him. I know he wonders if he really is being sent visions from God. The Sheriff, on the other hand—'

'Thinks he's simply insane?'

'Yes, Little Flower.' Tuck regarded the figure on the floor. He was completely motionless, all the fight

75

from him now gone. 'Talking of which… he knew I called you "Little Flower", Marion. I know it sounds mad, but I feel like he knows me; that he knows *us*. Personally, I mean. He is known as the Magic Man.'

'Is he, indeed?' Will scoffed.

'Magic?' Much paled as Robin freed his ankles. 'Is he dangerous?'

'I don't think so,' Tuck said, pulling a face. 'But I can't be sure. I *am* certain he is trying to help, but it's like he doesn't know his own mind.'

'So, he *is* insane,' Will tutted. 'The Sheriff was right… much as it pains me to agree with that sorry excuse for a human being.'

'Why do *you* think we should trust this man, Tuck?' Robin asked gently.

'Because… um… I don't really know,' Tuck frowned. 'Instinct, maybe… and, well, because of him, we *are* all here together.'

'Yeah, tied up and held prisoner!' John muttered.

'And,' Will added, 'if you hadn't been so picky about not raiding an abbey, we'd all have been here together *anyway*, Tuck.'

Ignoring the inconvenient truths from John and Will, the friar unpicked the knots that held the Magic Man's wrists together. 'Can you tell me who you are?' he asked.

'I had a name once, but it's been an age since anyone used it. I've happily been known as Storyteller for so long… or, lately, Magic Man.' His words fractured and his head rolled from side to side as if he were trying to sort his thoughts rather than knock something dark from his mind.

'Are you alright?' Tuck glanced anxiously over the older man's shoulders, as his friends huddled around him.

'There's a mist—a new mist—a recent mist. It fills my mind. Sometimes it completely blocks my sight. Another puts it there; one who seeks to control me, to use my abilities, and…' He sat up abruptly, his brown eyes burning sapphire as words tumbled from his lips, abrupt and urgent. 'A wagon… here. *Now*. You must stop them. *Go!*'

Robin surveyed the dark room. 'Scarlet, did you see where they threw our weapons?'

'Yeah. Near the door. I'll get them.'

As Will retrieved their arms, Robin addressed the man on the floor, 'Come with us.'

'I am needed here. But I promise I will help you, Herne's Son.'

'How?'

'You will see.'

'But—'

John grabbed Robin's arm. 'We have to go. Let's grab as much food as we can carry and get out of here before the guard outside realises we're free.'

'No. Wait!' Tuck spun round and explained, 'There are mercenaries here. They broke in and demanded the food for themselves. *They* are the ones we must stop.'

'What?' Will grimaced. 'And when were you going to bother to tell us that?'

'I just did! And so did he... sort of.'

Robin took a deep breath, then asked, 'Tuck, is there anything else you can you tell us?'

'A mercenary came into the abbey. He told the Abbot and the Sheriff that if they didn't allow him and his men to fill a wagon full of food, they'd kill Gisburne.'

Scarlet's eyes widened. '*Gisburne* is here too? Oh this gets better and better.'

'The Abbot told me as we walked to the chapel together.'

'*And* you had a nice stroll with Abbot Hugo?' Will asked, incredulously.

Tuck glanced anxiously at the Magic Man. 'I'll tell you all about it later, but now we need to act.'

'You're right,' Robin said, swiftly issuing out instructions. 'Nasir, John, Will; we'll deal with the guards and lead the way out. Marion, Much, Tuck; get yourselves ready to follow us so we can face these mercenaries together.'

'How many are there going to be?'

'I don't know, Much, but we need to be prepared for—' Robin stopped talking as a sharp pain pulsed between his eyes and his body froze to the spot.

'Robin?' Marion rushed forwards as her husband sagged in pain. 'What is it? What's wrong?'

With one hand on his head, his eyes screwed shut, Robin murmured, 'Five men, armed with knives... plus a rider driving the horse and wagon and a bowman hides in the trees.'

Joining Marion at Robin's side as he abruptly stopped talking and opened his eyes, Little John asked, 'What happened? Was that Herne?'

'I don't know... it didn't *feel* like Herne,' Robin said. Running both palms over his face, his body unclenched itself with a ragged exhalation of air. 'I saw it all! I—' He stopped mid-sentence, turned to the Magic Man and asked, 'Was that you?'

'I said I'd help you.'

As Robin nodded, Will came to his side too. 'What's going on?'

'We've been shown where our enemy is.'

Will, however, was unconvinced. 'Oh yeah, and

we can trust him to have shown you the truth, can we? He could be anyone.'

'I could be,' the Magic Man said as he lifted himself up so that he was now resting on one elbow. 'In fact, you are right, Will Scarlet. I *am* just anyone. I'm an ordinary person; one of thousands living from day to day. An ordinary man with an ordinary life.'

Tuck shook his head. 'You *aren't* though, are you? Not if you are seeing—and sharing—these visions.'

'Come off it, Tuck!' Will snapped. 'He's just a charlatan, a—'

'Stop!' The sharp order stilled Scarlet's words on his tongue as every head turned to look towards the Magic Man. 'It does not matter who I am, nor how I see what I see, but if you do not act now, you *will* miss the chance to feed your people.'

CHAPTER TEN

'You say you will help make me powerful, yet you teach me no magic; you give me no useful information. Since I arrived, I have simply stood in this impossible space and watched you stir that twig in that bowl.'

Elis didn't falter in his task, only saying, 'Impatience will be the death of you if you are not careful.'

'I have promised to help you, but if you do not help *me*, then…'

The druid dropped the twig and clapped his hands together so hard and so fast that his uninvited guest blinked; the blink turned to terrified awe as he watched Elis slowly part his hands again, forming a cloud of dust between them—dust that certainly hadn't been there before.

'What is that?'

'It is your mind, your thoughts. So crowded are they by your ambition that you are not ready for the help you seek. Since you walked into my home, you have craved the ability to perform magic—to master witchcraft, sorcery, alchemy—call it what you will.'

'I certainly have not! That is—'

'Beneath you as a nobleman?'

He looked startled. 'I—'

'You consistently forget that I can read your mind… even the parts of it that you have not yet seen for yourself.' Elis lowered his hands, making the dust fog vanish as he picked his twig up. 'When your mind is clearer, I will share what magical knowledge I can. *If* you can keep your patience.'

Irritably tugging a stray twig from his hair, Sir Guy of Gisburne crawled towards the abbey's gatehouse. He could feel the damp forest floor seeping through the knees of his breeches, and knots of exposed tree roots scratched at his hands.

The mercenary who'd been left to guard him had been ridiculously easy to subdue.

'If he'd worked for me at the castle, he wouldn't have lasted five minutes,' Gisburne grumbled as he shuffled nearer to the abbey.

He could already hear the other mercenaries. They thought they were being quiet, but their self-congratulatory plans on how much they were going to be eating or drinking by midnight was carried on the evening air with a crisp clarity. He grinned to himself.

The fools think they're untouchable just because they look tough. If only they stopped to think, they'd remember just how far sound travels in the forest.

A cruel smile crossed his face. *They have courage though... and muscle. Perhaps I could use them.* His smiled widened further as a new, more obvious ambition hit him. *I will make them work for me— show them how much better they'd be with me in charge.*

'Once I'm leading them, they'll have to be a lot more careful though,' he muttered to himself.

Rising up a fraction so he was now crouched on his haunches, Gisburne stole forwards again, and saw what he'd previously only heard. Five men had formed a chain, moving food from the abbey to the wagon—food that was being handed over by some frightened looking monks.

Five men... plus one on the wagon. But seven men left the camp, so where is the other one?

In his head, Gisburne pictured the abbey's larder. *He's probably inside holding a monk hostage so they all do as they are told.*

A malevolent grin crossed his face as he muttered, 'Hmm, unless he has the Abbot—or the Sheriff—held under the blade of his knife.'

No. If they were the ones in trouble, some hapless soldiers would already be out here getting themselves killed trying to protect their masters. He shook his head. *So where ARE the Abbot and the Sheriff?*

'Hah! They're either too cowardly to try and stop this, or too drunk to even notice it's happening,' Gisburne grumbled under his breath as he observed the mercenaries in action.

When the wagon was almost full, the felon nearest to him—whom he recognised as the one they'd called Brandon—shouted, 'Three more loads, then we leave!'

Immediately, the cutthroats sped up, throwing the goods they held along the line.

Gisburne clambered to his feet. The man who'd been left to guard him had clearly been the runt of the litter. *These* men, however, knew what they were doing. They had style and nerve, and worked well together. If they had the right leader they'd be capable of anything.

They need me.

A new sound reached his ears. Faint. It was hardly a sound at all, more a vibration of the ground beneath his feet. Gisburne grasped his sword's handle as a figure he recognised flitted through the shadows ahead of him; he held a longbow in one hand and an arrow in the other.

'Hood!'

'Why didn't you leave with your friends?'

Friar Tuck sat down next to the Magic Man and answered, 'I don't know. I just had a feeling that you needed me to stay.'

'I see.'

'You do, don't you? In more ways than one.' Tuck's hand wrapped around the cross he wore beneath his robes, and as he held it tight, he finally asked the question he'd been wanting to. 'You really *do* see visions?'

'I truly thought God had blessed me... or cursed me; I wasn't sure which, Brother. But now I know differently. One who I thought had given up on hounding my existence has found me. They are affecting my mind.'

'Affecting it? How?'

'He is tapping into my own prophecies.'

'But your visions are helpful, aren't they? You saw the mercenaries, you sent Robin to stop them.' A cold sweat broke out on Tuck's forehead as he asked, 'Didn't you?'

'Yes. I did. The pictures I'm seeing are like the thoughts I had before—thoughts that can help people. But he is now using them to break into my mind, to track me.'

'So… each time you have a vision, he can see where you are more clearly?'

'I believe so, yes.'

'And this person… *why* would they go to all this trouble?'

'Revenge Brother Tuck, simple revenge.'

Gisburne knew this was his chance, and if he were to take it, it was now or never. His ego, as ever, overrode his rationality.

This is it. I'll warn the mercenaries that Robin Hood is here. They'll have to let me join them. They'll see I'm the better choice as leader. Then, I'll turn them into my expendable soldiers to kill Hood! That way, I claim the glory, as I can say I did it and easily arrest these fools. It's the perfect plan! I just need to gain their trust first, above all else…

Keeping his voice low, he let out a low hiss to attract Brandon's attention, 'Psst!'

The mercenary turned, a puzzled furrow appearing on his forehead as he scanned for the source of the noise.

Waving a hand, Gisburne enjoyed the stunned recognition on the man's face, but put a finger to his lips, suggesting he should remain silent as he beckoned for him to approach.

Brandon gestured to his nearest companion to keep watch and—holding his knife out before him, making it clear he was aiming it at Gisburne—he sidled forwards, asking, 'How did *you* get free?'

'Easily; the man you left me with was a halfwit,' Gisburne whispered. 'He isn't worthy to be part of your group.'

The man's eyebrows rose so high they were almost hidden by his mop of black curls. 'Did you kill him?'

'No, there was no need to go that far,' Gisburne grimaced. 'You deserve more capable men or you'll be captured in no time.'

'But how did you get free?'

'When I join you, I'll tell you my secret. For now, let us just say I talked myself to safety... delivering a punch as I left,' Gisburne smiled suggestively. '*I* would never have left anyone so gullible in charge of a prisoner. We should talk about how to improve things before we leave Sherwood.'

'*We?*'

'Weren't you listening? I've decided to join you. It's clear you need better leadership.'

Incredulous, Brandon was about to burst out laughing, but Gisburne, impervious to the felon's disbelief, hadn't finished.

'You are being watched. By outlaws. They intend to take the wagon.'

Instantly on guard, the mercenary twisted around intending to alert his men, but there was no time for words. An arrow made Gisburne's point perfectly for him, as—after slicing through the air— it landed in the side of the wagon with a thrumming thud.

'Warning shot!' Gisburne shouted as he dived downwards.

Brandon hit the ground beside him and muttered, 'It's alright. They don't know we have an archer in the—'

An anguished scream cut him off, as the man in question fell from the tree in which he'd been hiding, an arrow planted firmly in his chest.

'How did they know he was there?'

Gisburne gritted his teeth. 'I hate them, but they are good at what they do. And they sometimes have help—magical help... or so they claim.'

'You don't believe in magic?'

'No, I don't. I believe in clever men who know how to manipulate the facts to make them seem more than they are. These outlaws,' Gisburne spat, 'are nothing more than homeless criminals.'

The mercenary glared, 'Be careful, nobleman, the same could be said about us.'

Gisburne swallowed the lump that had formed in his throat. 'There is a good deal of difference between you and that Wolfshead.'

'Yes, there is,' the man scowled. 'If they really *are* Hood's men, then *they* give their money away. We do *not!*'

Keeping his eyes fixed on the wagon ahead, waiting for the outlaws to show themselves, Gisburne ignored the cold sweat that had broken out on his neck, and continued making his point, 'Which just goes to show how stupid they are.'

'And yet you are afraid of them.'

'I am afraid of no one!' Gisburne growled, anger tearing at him. 'And as you haven't ordered your men forwards to stop them taking the wagon, then it appears that *you* are the one who is afraid!'

CHAPTER ELEVEN

'Where the hell is Tuck?'

Robin spun round to face Will. 'I thought he was behind you,' he exclaimed.

'So did I.'

Marion peered anxiously across to where the wagon was waiting. 'Maybe he followed Nasir, Much and John to help surround the mercenaries from the other side.'

'He better have,' Will steamed.

'Well, there's no time to wait. We need to act now.' Robin felt an image forming on the inside of his mind, and the headache, which had overpowered him before, nudged at his temples.

Not now... I need to concentrate.

Suddenly, as if the cause of the ache had heard

and understood him, his mind lightened. Yet as he pulled back his bow again, he found that he knew exactly where Tuck was.

'He's with the Magic Man,' Robin said.

'What?' Will's temper was close to breaking. 'We need his help *here.*'

'We'll manage,' Marion spoke fast, trying to placate the situation as Robin rose a hand to indicate to their friends across the clearing that the time had come to attack.

'Ready?'

With a muted chorus of "Ready" from Marion and Will, the outlaws emerged from the trees from all sides, quickly surrounding the cart.

'Put down your weapons!' Robin called, but rather than obeying, the mercenaries collectively drew their swords; their expressions hardened as they regarded the outlaws.

'Your archer is dead and those swords are useless against our arrows,' said Robin. 'You will leave now… *without* the cart. If you haven't gone by the time Scarlet here has counted to ten, then I will be forced to break a promise I've made and kill on holy ground.'

'You already have, you coward!'

'No, I have not.'

'*I have,*' Nasir said as he stepped over the body of the mercenary archer. 'To me, this is no holy ground.'

'You have no respect for—'

'Nor have you, stealing from an abbey,' Will snarled.

'You are stealing from it too!'

'We are not,' Robin countered, holding the gaze of the man he took to be the mercenaries' leader. '*We* are taking back what was stolen in order to return it to its rightful owners.'

Gisburne grabbed hold of Brandon's arm as they watched Robin Hood attack. 'It's no good trying to help; the outlaws will win.'

'And here's you saying *we* are the cowards!'

'Shh,' Gisburne snarled, 'they have your men surrounded. If you want to give them both a living and food tonight then come with me.'

'Where to?'

'They can't have loaded *all* of the food onto the cart, and there won't be any guards watching the larder now as they'll have noticed the outlaws have escaped, so...'

'Let's go and grab what's left.'

'Exactly.'

'For how long have you experienced these visions?' Tuck asked, finding a jug of ale and passing it to the Magic Man.

'Like the ones I'm having now? About a month. Before, I could work out events in advance... generally by calculated logic and careful thought. I mostly *felt* how things would go, only seeing images occasionally... and even then the images would be hazy at best. But now, when a vision comes, it is clear and precise. And it's as if I'm there too, hovering over what I witness—seeing while being unseen.'

'You gave Robin a vision, didn't you?'

'I did—and that's a new thing. I don't know how I do that. Beyond thinking it would be useful, I sort of... know I have to help... as helping is...' His eyes dulled. 'I have been told to help, I'm sure I must have been... but then, I'd help anyway, so...'

'But if you are certain your thoughts have been invaded by someone out for revenge, why would they want you to be helping others?'

'I do not know. I only know that I can't trust *all* I see. I wonder if I'm being tricked into helping. I am aware this doesn't make sense...'

The Magic Man's words trailed off as he fell into his own thoughts, sending a new wave of unease through Tuck.

'Do you have a name?' asked the friar. '"Magic Man" is the kind of title that invites trouble.'

'That it is, Brother,' the Magic Man agreed. Dragging himself from his internal battle, he took a swig of ale. 'Only in the last month has that name fallen on me. I have occasionally been called "Soothsayer" in the past—but affectionately, perhaps when I've worked out a pattern of events. I myself prefer "Storyteller".'

Tuck tilted his head to one side. 'I'm sure you do, but that is not what I meant. Do you have a first name? Are you David, or Edwin or—'

Suddenly, the Magic Man's hand shot out and caught Tuck's wrist. His eyes glazed over and his breathing became laboured as a new vision clearly began to sweep over him. Keeping a tight hold of the friar's arm, he murmured, 'Close your eyes; *you* must see this too.'

Alarmed at the urgency in his companion's voice, Tuck did as he was bidden. He gasped as pictures formed in his head, images over which he had no control.

'Tell me what you see, Brother Tuck.'

An abrupt headache washed over the friar. 'Gisburne... he's approaching the abbey's larder. He's not alone—he's with a mercenary, I think. They are taking the food sacks...' Tuck was about to break away from the Magic Man when the scene altered rapidly. Now he could see Robin talking to the Magic Man—and then it changed again and he saw Gisburne in the forest. Suddenly, again with no warning, a mountain range broke into the vision... and there was... blood.

Tuck abruptly pulled away, crying, 'Blood—blood on bread.' Gathering himself together, he made for the door. 'I must tell Robin and the others that Gisburne—'

'No.'

'No?' Tuck wondered at the Magic Man's commanding tone.

'Sir Guy *must* take the food sacks.'

'But the people need—'

The Magic Man's eyes blazed their sapphire blue. 'I have seen that this is what has to be.'

Tuck paused, before saying what was on his mind, 'Can I *trust* you, Storyteller?'

The now thankfully-less-possessed man gave Tuck a sad smile. 'As much as I trust myself, yes.'

'In the vision, I saw you with Robin.'

'You trust Herne's Son, don't you?'

'Yes, I do.'

'Then that will tell you all you need to know.'

'And there were mountains.'

The Magic Man nodded. 'Far away... that is where he is.'

'Who?'

'The one who seeks me.'

Tuck pulled his hood over his head against the growing nighttime chill. 'Tell me, who is he?'

'It is best if I do not; he can read minds.'

'But there was blood?'

'There will always be bloodshed in your story, Brother Tuck. Always.'

Gisburne hadn't been able to believe his luck when he'd found some sacks inside the larder's doorway. Assuming they were what the outlaws had intended to use to carry away supplies, he and Brandon had filled as many as they could carry.

Expecting a warm welcome from the men he was already allowing himself to think of as his followers, his assassins, Gisburne stomped confidently through a stretch of outlaw-free woodland, just ahead of Brandon, entering the mercenaries' camp without a hint of caution.

On arrival however, he found a very different welcome from the one his rampant, delusional ego had imagined.

'Brandon, where have you been?' The chief mercenary's voice was merciless.

'Getting the food we needed, Cedric.'

'With him? Our prisoner?'

Brandon held out the two bulging sacks of food he held in his hands. 'We saw you were surrounded. If we had tried to help, we would certainly have been shot. So, we went to—'

It was too much for Gisburne. Breaking in before the other man could take credit for his idea, he barked, 'We went to the abbey's larder. I led the way. If it wasn't for me—'

'If it wasn't for you, Sheriff's boy, then we would not have lost one of our number to an outlaw's arrow,' yelled Cedric.

'I am not responsible for his death!'

Glaring angrily at Gisburne, Cedric spat, 'You

98

are a target for Hood's men. We all know the stories! He'd never have bothered with us if you hadn't stolen the food from the people in the first place. We could have gone into the abbey's larder, got what we wanted, and Hood would never have been nearby in the first place.'

'But you only know about the abbey because of me. You wouldn't have any of this without my help!'

'Andrew would be alive though.'

'And you'd be hungry! Why bleat over a dead man?'

Brandon turned on Gisburne with such speed that his boots churned up the earth beneath his feet. 'He was our friend.'

Incomprehension flooded Gisburne. 'But you're mercenaries,' he cried.

'And we are loyal to each other,' Brandon said, dropping the sacks he carried. 'If you don't understand loyalty, Gisburne—' he flicked his knife from his belt, holding it out before him, '—then you won't be joining us at all, let alone leading us.'

'Leading us?' The chief mercenary tugged his own dagger free and tossed it from hand to hand, clearly grandstanding. 'Brandon, I think you need to tell us what our visitor here has been saying while you were also failing to rescue us from the outlaws.'

Suddenly unsure, Brandon turned to his original leader and argued, 'I was ensuring we had some food—this man is right about one thing; we couldn't have saved you. And Gisburne was certain the outlaws wouldn't hurt anyone once they had what they wanted.'

'But they killed Andrew!'

'I wish they had not,' Brandon said, lowering his head, 'but we could not have stopped that. None of us could.'

'That's as maybe… but tell me, Brandon,' Cedric swung around to face Gisburne, 'what do you have to say about this noble fool wanting to replace me as leader?'

'I am no fool,' spat Sir Guy.

'Yet you think you can arrive here as our prisoner and then—within a few hours no less—take over and become the leader of this group? My group? A group that has always been loyal to me… until now!' Cedric spun back to face Brandon. 'Do you have anything to say about that?'

'I would never—'

'And yet you let this man lead you to the abbey's larder.'

'For us. For food.'

Cedric grabbed Brandon by the beard and

tugged his face closer so they were eye-to-eye. 'Must I question your loyalty?'

'No! I was using his knowledge to our advantage, that is all.'

'Then prove it.'

'I already have proven it! The food we gathered is here. I am here. And this fool,' Brandon stabbed a finger at Gisburne, 'is nothing.'

'Fool?' Rage swam in Gisburne's gut. 'I told you; I am not a fool! And I'm better to lead these men that you are!' he said, turning to face Cedric. 'I'm the Sheriff of Nottingham's deputy! I am in charge of this whole shire when he is away. I am trusted with—'

The swipe of a gloved hand hit Gisburne across the face with sharp accuracy, making him groan in pain and his eyes water. 'How dare you?' he spluttered.

Cedric drew his blade from his belt.

'Easily.'

CHAPTER TWELVE

His eyes stung from staring at the pictures that painted themselves over the bowl's rippling blue liquid. 'Elis, why do you show me the Sheriff's underling? The mercenaries speak the truth. He *is* a fool.'

'This is foreknowledge. It will be useful for your future, dyn drwg. I promised—did I not—to show you all I could to ease your way to power?'

'You did.' He faltered, and forced out an apology, 'I'm sorry. I grew impatient.'

Elis gave him a shrewd stare. 'Perhaps you *are* able to learn after all.'

'And this man…'

'Sir Guy of Gisburne.'

'This knight then; what will he be to me?'

'To many he is a piece of grit in their boot; an annoyance that won't seem to go away—although he does try to leave, every so often….' Elis broke off as a phlegm-filled cough punctuated his speech. He spat a slimy deposit of green gunk into the corner before he returned to stirring the willow twig, now sending the liquid in the bowl a deep purple. 'A minor player in your game,' he continued, 'but we all require such deluded underlings to forge our path.'

'And this particular one—why might I need him?'

'Because this knight will provide you with a mind that is easy to mould to your desires, should you need a pair of ambitious hands. And, more importantly, because he hates Herne's Son… just as you will one day.'

'I will?'

'Without a doubt.'

'So, I should find a way to kill him now?'

Elis experienced an unexpected sense of disgust as he regarded his guest. 'The shine of pleasure in your eyes at the thought of murder is not a pleasant one, dyn drwg. It is also redundant. Killing Herne's Son will not rid you of Herne's Son.'

'That makes no sense at all. You've already spoken about me killing your so-called Magic Man.'

'There is a reason for that.'

The noble thought carefully. 'The Magic Man is helping Herne's Son. If I destroy him, are you saying that—by doing so—I will get the measure of men who try to block my way in the future.'

'Exactly that. And, if you use the power I teach you carefully, then the outlaws will get the blame for the Magic Man's death.'

'Does this mean you *will* give me some magical ability, so I can—'

'When it is necessary to do so, yes,' the druid confirmed, wiping a grubby hand over his tired face and streaking it with smuts of soot. 'Now, watch the drama unfold.'

Sweat dripped off Tuck's tonsure as he hurtled between the trees.

Please be at the camp, please be at the camp...

He ran the words through his head like a monk's chant as he wove between the trees. Tuck knew that—despite the lateness of the hour—there was a good chance his friends would go straight to Wickham or to one of the other villages from which the Sheriff had taken a food tithe, in order to return what had been stolen.

It's late... surely they'll go home to rest.

With the vision he'd seen still sending tremors of disquiet through his corpulent frame, he puffed onwards.

'I must speak to Robin. I must warn him...'

'To the right.' Nasir stopped moving and pointed into the trees. 'Men. At least five.'

'Those trees are thick; we'll never get through without getting the wagon stuck.' Will said, resting against the nearest tree.

'We could go around the other side,' said Much. 'I knows this bit of the forest; it's more open if we take the left path and circle round.'

'You're right,' Robin agreed, 'but I'd like to see what we are facing before we risk being spotted.'

'I'd fit through there.' Marion tapped the nearest tree in the thicket. 'I could find out what is going on.'

'Good idea.' Robin squeezed her hand, before adding, 'But be careful.'

Only stopping to roll her eyes at his unneeded caution, Marion crept forwards. Taking her time, she made her way towards the sounds they'd heard. Only a few paces later, she came to a halt before retracing her steps with speed.

'It's the mercenaries from whom we took the wagon,' she explained, then turning to Robin, added, 'Tuck was right; they have Gisburne at the end of a dagger... the sharp end.' Marion grimaced. 'He looks frightened. These are not good men.'

Will grunted, 'Then I say we should leave them to it.'

'Scarlet!' Robin shook his head. 'You know we can't just leave him at their mercy.'

'Why not?' Will scowled. 'If he found you in there with that lot, he'd happily settle down to watch you get skewered.'

'I've told you before, we are better than that.'

Will grunted for a second time. 'Maybe. Sometimes.'

'Did you see anything else, lass?' Little John interjected before Robin and Will's disagreement could grow into a full-blown argument.

'Yes. They used our sacks to get more food, by the looks of it. I could see four, and they were definitely all full.'

'Then we take those as well,' Robin said, sliding Albion from his belt.

'As well as what?' Will's eyes narrowed.

'Gisburne.'

'Oh for God's sake,' Will spluttered. 'How many times are we going to—'

'Someone comes!' Nasir interrupted, sending the outlaws diving into the trees, only to reappear as a familiar figure bustled towards them.

'Hello, Tuck,' Much beamed as the friar wheezed to a stop.

'Robin,' Tuck puffed, leaning forwards, 'the Magic Man showed me a vision. But he thinks... he thinks someone is controlling the things he sees.'

'Controlling them how?'

'I don't know, but not from Sherwood. There were mountains.'

'Mountains?' Marion queried. 'Welsh mountains? Scottish? French?'

'No idea. All I do know is that we can only trust what he sees to a certain extent.'

'Hmm.' Robin tried to think. 'He *was* right about the mercenaries stealing the food with a wagon, though.'

'He was. But each time he has a vision, the person who is watching him can see him more clearly.'

'And so ultimately find him?' Nasir suggested, his eyes narrowing.

'Exactly.'

Robin asked urgently, 'Tuck, what did he say he saw about Gisburne?'

'Gisburne took the sacks we were going to use. He filled them with food. But I don't know where he planned to take them.'

'We do,' Will muttered as he stabbed a finger to the camp hidden between the trees.

'Closer,' Elis commanded, gripping his companion's robes in a gnarled fist and urging him so near to the fire and the bowl balanced over it that sparks of heat singed his breeches.

He said nothing as he watched.

'You see them, dyn drwg, in one form or other. These people mark your rise to power.'

Gisburne was having to remind himself to breathe. His world was currently very small, consisting only of the glint of the dagger and that in the eyes of the mercenaries now surrounding him.

'You appear to be significantly less confident than you were before, Sir Guy,' Cedric mocked as he slapped the flat of his dagger against his prisoner's neck. 'Do you still have plans to take my place as leader?'

'I found you all that food.'

'And that's your response, is it? Reminding us that you filled a few sacks with bread while we faced death?' Furious, Cedric broke away, grabbing one of the food bags and emptying it out on the forest floor, before whirling back round and returning the blade to his captive's throat.

Gisburne gulped. 'If a leader was needed, I could lead here. But, clearly... it isn't. If I was in charge, I would have posted lookouts around this camp. We are in Sherwood after all, and—'

Cedric punched Gisburne hard in the stomach with his free hand. 'We are not like you,' he spat. 'We aren't sacred of a few tatty outlaws.'

'You were just now,' Gisburne groaned through his pain.

Cedric's eyes flashed with menace. 'I can't decide

if you are extremely stupid or extremely brave for saying that.'

Scowling at the chief mercenary, Gisburne spoke through gritted teeth as he held his hands over his aching stomach, 'I wouldn't have said I would take charge here had Brandon not suggested it was a good idea.'

'I never said—'

Brandon's words died on his lips as Cedric hurled himself forwards, shouting, 'You traitor!'

'I didn't… I didn't… Ahh!'

A dagger slipped deep into the flesh of Brandon's shoulder. Cedric radiated anger as he pulled it out again, leaving his fellow mercenary writhing on the ground amongst the fallen food while his blood dripped from the weapon.

'Next time it will be your heart that gets skewered.'

Breaking his cover, Robin's shout of "There won't be a next time" flew across the clearing.

'Wolfshead,' Gisburne moaned in humiliation.

'You do seem to get yourself into a lot of trouble, Gisburne,' Robin said as his friends emerged from the trees, their longbows armed and drawn. 'And it appears,' he turned to Cedric, 'that *you* do not learn. We surrounded you like this merely hours ago, but still you have no men watching out for trouble, even though you are in our forest.'

Gisburne couldn't help himself. 'That's what *I* said they should do!'

'Shut up, Gisburne,' Will snarled as he saw the mercenaries fix questioning gazes upon their leader.

'Tuck,' Robin called, then gestured towards Brandon. 'This man is wounded. Will you see if he can be helped?'

'Certainly,' agreed the friar, lowering his bow and arrow. Ignoring the mercenary's look of surprise, Tuck ran a gentle hand over his shoulder before examining the wound. 'It's deep… but it will heal.'

'Good.' Robin kicked a lose stone across the ground. 'Get out of here, Gisburne. The Sheriff will be looking for you.'

'And think yourself lucky to be alive… again!' growled Will.

As Gisburne rose unsteadily to his feet, Robin added, 'If you even think about bringing any guards into the forest to find us tonight, you will not live to tell anyone about it later.'

The sound of Gisburne's fleeing footfall faded as Robin spoke again, 'Much, Marion, gather up the three other sacks. These men can have the one they've spilled. Everyone needs *some* food, after all.'

As the two outlaws darted forwards to collect the food from the floor, Tuck helped Brandon to sit upright. A second later the cleric's face went a deathly pale.

'Tuck?' John moved forwards. 'What is it?'

The friar pointed to the tumble of bread that had been thrown from the sack and simply said, 'the Magic Man.'

The outlaws and mercenaries exchanged puzzled looks.

'I saw it. That there—he showed me in a vision. Brandon's blood has dripped onto the bread. *Blood on bread.*'

CHAPTER THIRTEEN

'This is all your fault, Hugo,' Robert de Rainault said, rounding on his brother. 'If you hadn't been so sure that lunatic was receiving messages from the Almighty, then he would be in Nottingham dungeon by now... and I would be in my castle eating roast pheasant!'

'If *you* hadn't been greedy and insisted on taking extra food from the people, then we wouldn't be in this mess in the first place, Robert... so don't you dare blame me!'

Ignoring the accusation, the Sheriff changed the subject. 'And where the hell is Gisburne? If he isn't back by morning, I'll have to return to Nottingham without him.'

'You care about Gisburne now, do you? Now

you've realised how dangerous it is to ride through Sherwood without him?'

'Do shut up, Hugo!' commanded the Sheriff, who peered miserably into the roaring fire before getting to his feet and continuing, 'I might as well go and check on our prisoners, seeing as you haven't even had the good grace to offer me a bed for the night yet!'

'You know where the guest chamber is, Robert!' Hugo yelled as his brother marched through the room's open door. 'It's hardly worth going to bed now, anyway.'

The Sheriff had no sooner disappeared from his sight than Abbot Hugo heard a cry that sent him racing after his brother.

'What do you mean they're gone? You idiot!'

A red faced guard stood trembling before his master. 'I was on my way to tell you, my Lord Sheriff. I went to relieve the guard on watch, but I found him unconscious and the outlaws gone.' He risked looking at the abbot. 'The other prisoner is still there, my Lords.'

'What do I care about that madman? If I'd captured Robin Hood, the King would have—'

'I'm sorry, my Lord Sheriff, I—'

Robert de Rainault's palm met the soldier's cheek with a solid slap. 'Don't you dare interrupt me! Now, get yourself into Sherwood and find Gisburne.'

'Into Sherwood, my Lord?'

'Yes. Now! And when you find Sir Guy, tell him if he isn't back here by dawn, his life won't be worth living.'

As the hapless guard scooted off, Abbot Hugo muttered, 'What makes you think Gisburne's life was worth living anyway?'

Snorting by way of a reply, the Sheriff strode towards the larder. 'I want to talk to this so-called Magic Man. He was in there with the outlaws; the chances are, he helped them escape.'

'Are you ready to do your first magic, dyn drwg?'

He looked up sharply. 'Really?'

'You came here searching for power, asking me for a way to get what you deserve. I thought magic was what you wanted.'

'Yes. Yes it is.'

'Well then. I use the old ways to get what I want. Scrying, magic, words, the willow… natures magic. I have shown you many of the players in the game. Characters that form the bedrock of your future story. The others—there are five more men in your tale—you have met before, bar one. This final player you will meet by chance and as yet the mist is still too thick to reveal him to me. But he will be revealed when the time is right for you… in….' He paused, squeezing his eyes closed and clutching his twig tighter in his fist. '…in a village… yes… a village.'

'Why would I ever go to a village?'

Elis reopened his eyes. 'Why would you ever come to the mountains, nobleman?'

He conceded the point, 'To get what I want.'

'Precisely. You will know which village when the time is right.'

'These four men I've met before. Which four?' He frowned, a familiar sense of frustration coming over him. 'I know many men. How can I know—'

'You will know when you are supposed to! That time is not now.' Elis spat into the bowl before continuing, 'However, if you act now—and succeed—then these other men's roles will not be required; their stanzas in your ballad will remain unwritten. But, if you fail now, all is not lost, and you will encounter these men in the future, knowing how you must face them.'

'You speak in circles. How can I trust you will help me when you say we might fail—and then tease me with a backup plan?'

'Is it not better that I am honest? This Hooded Man is never to be underestimated.'

Feeling his temper fray, he gritted his teeth together. 'But you are a Fferyllt! History shows the Fferyllt are undefeated. Their magic is—'

'*Was!*' Elis flexed the willow twig menacingly between his palms. 'He could have saved us. Returned us to the supremacy we enjoyed before. But he didn't... he wouldn't.'

'What do you mean?'

'Our numbers were dwindling—and then our most influential brother died. We searched the length of England, Scotland and Wales for another to fill the void. After two years of hunting we found one who could join us—one skilled enough to take our brother's place.'

'This so-called Magic Man?'

'Indeed. But he refused. He disappeared, deliberately hiding himself from our reach. We sought him anyway, but his ability to block us was faultless.'

'But you *have* found him?'

'Age weakens the human in so many ways. Only now—some twenty years later—did I locate a chink in his armour.'

He took a wary step away from Elis as he ventured, 'If this man can save your kind, then why do you want me to kill him?'

'Because it is too late. I am now the *only one* left of my kind. His refusal to help saw our demise. He destroyed my kin. And so, before I reach my own death, I will see him destroyed.'

'Yet it isn't you who intends to remove this Magic Man from the earth; you order *me* to eliminate him.'

'A fair price for my help.'

'Only if you give me what I ask for! You have just told me your plan to help me might not work this time around, that I may have to wait far longer to seize what I deserve!'

A hacking cough overtook Elis before he could respond. When he did, his voice was subdued, 'I did not foresee Herne's Son's involvement at this stage of your story; I saw him later in your tale!'

'But you see into the future! You should have known—you should have seen!'

'Listen,' Elis hissed, slapping the twig so hard against the side of the bowl that it vibrated with an angry hum around the cramped, stone-lined, space, 'I am a Fferyllt! I am Elis the Druid! But there are some who have found a way to interfere.' His frustrated ire dropped to a simmer of hate. 'Some, like Herne the Hunter, have found a way to block us, hide themselves from us—to protect the realms they lord it over from us… from me. They blur the accuracy of the future I see.'

Thrusting the twig into the bowl, Elis watched as the pool of blue liquid shone up at him like an enticing sapphire. 'For some time, I've wondered if the Magic Man had aligned himself with others to keep hidden. And now Herne's Son has appeared in my pool—as have you, dyn drwg.'

Though straightening in offence, the nobleman nonetheless spoke cautiously, 'I had never heard of Herne's Son or even Herne before I came here. Why would I have?'

'The stories of Robin Hood are—'

'Yes, yes… the outlaws are sung of when men are drunk and feeble-minded… but not this spirit whom you tell me guides him.'

The druid's face contorted with suspicion. 'Are you sure?'

'I've heard no word of this spirit before. I swear.'

'Interesting,' Elis said as he drummed the twig thoughtfully against the stone wall, 'there may yet be a way.'

'A way for what?'

'Your time has come, dyn drwg.' The druid abruptly held out the twig. 'Take this. You are going to give the Magic Man a vision.'

CHAPTER FOURTEEN

Although disappointed to find the outlaws gone, neither of the de Rainault brothers were surprised. Yet, this fact didn't stop the Sheriff wanting to blame someone else for this latest failure to remove Herne's Son from the world.

'You!' the Sheriff shouted, focusing his ire on the solitary figure left in the rectory. 'You let them go!'

'I did not.'

The Magic Man's tranquil tone did nothing to calm the Sheriff's anger.

'So, they just undid their ties and walked out on their own, did they?'

'I believe the Lady Marion managed to slip her bindings. Then she freed her friends. And freed me.' He held up his wrists. 'The outlaws asked me to go with them, but my work here is not yet done, and so I remain.'

'What work?' Abbot Hugo put a restraining hand on his brother's shoulder. 'Explain.'

'You have a tolerance—even a certain acceptance and understanding—of magic, Abbot. Anyone who walks the line of religion needs such knowledge, even if all it does is make them disbelieve in its influence. You, however, Sheriff,' he fixed his hazel eyes on Robert de Rainault, 'you dismiss it without thinking. You refuse to see magic even when it is directly in front of your eyes. You declare Herne a madman; you see me as insane. My message for you is both simple and vital to your future existence. Magic is real. It crackles in the earth and sings through the trees. But most of all, it is in the language and the stories. Shun the tales of the people, my Lords, and you will be victims of the power of their words for the rest of your days.'

'What idiocy!'

'You prove my point for me, Sheriff.' Turning to the abbot, the Magic Man smiled, 'I thank you for your sanctuary. Whilst in the chapel, I was hidden from danger; I could control what I saw—now...' He launched out a hand and seized hold of Hugo, '...you will see.'

The Abbot sagged at the knees as pictures flashed through his mind. 'What's happening? I—'

'Relax... I'm sharing what I see with you. Look.... *Look...*'

Hugo closed his eyes, blocking out the sneer of contempt on his brother's face.

'It's Gisburne, he's... wait... he's with the mercenary we saw and... he's on his knees... there's a knife at his throat. I think they are going to kill—'

There was a strangled cry from the Magic Man, who instantly dropped the abbot's arm and fell to his knees. A fog swirled through his mind, obscuring the vision he shared with Hugo and sending hot prickles of tension through his body before a new series of images crashed through his head in quick succession.

'Mountains... blood... blood on bread and...' The Magic Man coughed, his head light, his limbs weakening. 'He is using someone else to find me... a powerful man will die... the time is coming...'

With an extreme effort of will, the Magic Man tore himself from the vision. Laying on the floor, he gaped like a floundering fish while he recovered his senses.

'Well, that was a fine performance,' mocked the Sheriff with a slow handclap, 'worthy of those dreadful mummers the King likes to have prancing around at the Royal Court.'

Ignoring his brother, Hugo mumbled, 'I saw Gisburne.'

The Sheriff sneered, 'How lovely for you.'

'He's in trouble, Robert. There was a knife at his throat!'

'Gisburne is *always* in trouble! Trouble is his speciality!'

'What if *he's* the powerful man?' Hugo wiped the sleeve of his robes over his forehead. 'He could be dead already.'

'Gisburne is not a powerful man,' the Sheriff scoffed… then he paused, as he stared at the Magic Man. 'But if this idiot sees Guy as powerful—and if he *is* dead—that means that neither you, nor I, are the "powerful man" in question. Which means *we* are safe, Hugo.'

Muttering from his position on the stone floor, the Magic Man whispered, 'So… you believe in my visions when they might affect you personally, Sheriff, but you also choose to dismiss them when they do not come as close to touching your comfortable life. Interesting.'

Hugo sat heavily upon the nearest seat, looked at their prisoner and asked, 'What happened?'

'With the help of another, a man who has been searching for me for many years has found me.'

'That doesn't sound good.'

'It is not,' the Magic Man replied, smiling. 'I knew I was right to seek sanctuary.'

'Who has found you?'

'I do not know.'

The Sheriff rolled his eyes. 'How very convenient.'

'All I know is that it is one of the Fferyllt—a druid collective that lives in the mountains of Wales.'

'You said you saw mountains,' Hugo said as he leant forward in his chair.

'I did. While I was in your chapel, he could not reach me properly. But outside of its holy ground—'

'This *is* holy ground.' Hugo gestured around him.

'This is a food store. It is not a place holding an altar.'

The Sheriff glared at Abbot Hugo. 'I hate to interrupt this ridiculous conversation, but apparently Gisburne is dead—or almost dead—which means I must find myself a new deputy.'

'Robert, I just had a vision, and it might not—'

'Nonsense, it is all that claret catching up with you. It's getting late—or early. I'm going to bed, and then tomorrow I will return to Nottingham and talk to the Captain of the Guard about him taking over Gisburne's position.'

The nobleman gripped the side of the stone dish with his gloved hands. His breathing rasped in his throat as he tried to make sense of what had just happened. 'I made the Magic Man see things that he shared with the whining abbot.'

'You did. Then I added in a layer of my own, showing the Magic Man what I wanted him to see.' Elis smiled. 'I imagine he is rather scared... and scared men make mistakes, no matter how strong they are.'

The nobleman frowned. 'But we showed him things that have already happened. That man, Sir Guy of Gisburne, is not dead. He's not even a prisoner anymore. The outlaws have already let him go.'

'One thing at a time. First you will project recent events. When you have mastered that, then the future will be yours to see.'

'And to mould?'

'Eventually.'

The nobleman moved swiftly to the bowl's edge. 'Then let us continue with the lesson.'

Behind him, Elis gave a slow smile. 'Certainly, dyn drwg.'

The mercenaries... ... ...
... ...
... ...
... ...

CHAPTER FIFTEEN

Friar Tuck hadn't said a word since Robin had ordered the mercenaries to be on their way. Now, back at their own campfire, the heaviness of the friar's silence had become almost a physical presence.

'Tuck?' Marion finally broke the tension. 'What is it?'

'If I hadn't told Robin about what I'd seen, then Brandon would not have been wounded. It's only through pure luck that he's not dead.'

'But, by sharing what you saw, you may have saved his life. And you are probably the reason Gisburne isn't dead either; our arrival interrupted his execution.'

Tuck watched the dance of the fire's flames. 'But if we hadn't gone to the abbey in the first place—'

'Then the people of Sherwood wouldn't have enough food to last the season,' Robin said, gently. 'I did not ignore your feelings on this lightly, Tuck.'

'I know.'

Much peeped shyly at his friend. 'What was it like, seeing a vision?'

'It's hard to describe—like having a pounding headache while being shrouded in fog, and yet—at the same time—everything is as clear as a millpond. Like…'

'…a reflection of a reality to come,' Robin smiled.

'Exactly that, yes.' Tuck rose wearily to his feet. 'I am too tired to cook. If any of you are hungry, then you'll have to take something from the sacks the mercenaries filled. I'm going to bed.'

As Tuck bustled towards his favoured sleeping spot, just beyond his cooking pot, Much asked Robin, 'Is that how it feels when Herne shows you things?'

'Similar. I don't get a headache from Herne's prophecies though—well, only from trying to decipher them.'

'An' that causes all of us 'eadaches later.' Will Scarlet grumbled.

'Now *that* I can't argue with,' Robin laughed as he laid himself down next to the fire. 'Tomorrow we'll return the food to the villagers, but for now, I think we should all get some rest. Something tells me we haven't seen the last of this Magic Man yet.'

Sleep beckoned the outlaws, and they gave in to its calling, as—one by one—they fell into a slumber for the remaining few hours of darkness.

'Do you see them?'

'The outlaws, yes.' He peered into the blue liquid that bubbled over the fire with increased concentration. He could sense how close he was to everything he'd ever wanted. 'Will the Magic Man go to them?'

'They will meet.'

'You are sure?'

Elis's eye's narrowed. 'Either you trust me, or you don't.'

'Forgive me.' He dug his fingernails into his palms once more. 'Then what will happen?'

'You will kill him as you promised.'

'But I'm here.' The nobleman let his hungry gaze stray from the bowl and said, 'They are in Sherwood. Hundreds of miles away.'

'Did I say you would kill him *personally?*' Elis placed a single finger into the blue liquid and stirred it anticlockwise. 'Observe.'

Without hesitation, he obeyed. 'The outlaws sleep.'

'Yes.'

'Why do I need to watch a bunch of criminals in their slumber?'

'They—' A shadow crossed Elis's already line-crumpled face.

'What is it? What's wrong?'

'Nothing.' The druid gulped once, before recovering himself from the flash of future that had just invaded the recesses of his mind. 'Have you not been listening? These aren't just any outlaws; that is Robin Hood and his men, not to mention the Lady Marion.'

'I know who they are! We've spoken of them already. Besides, I told you, I've heard the stories.' He grunted. 'Didn't believe them, though.'

'And yet you now know they have the audacity to break into an abbey and steal food that had been taken from the poor.'

'I have seen this, yes.'

'Then you should believe the other stories. Stories are very important.'

'I've never bothered with them, myself.'

'And yet here you, dyn drwg.' Elis withdrew his finger from the liquid. It was bone dry. 'Did you not find me because of a tale that one guard told his bored comrade?'

'Well, yes. I suppose I did. I... How did you know that?'

Elis struck the willow twig against the bowl.

'Of course,' noted the nobleman. Heat infused the back of his neck as—for the first time—he allowed himself to contemplate how much power this druid truly wielded. 'For how long have you been watching me?'

'From the moment that guard mentioned the Fferyllt.'

'You heard that conversation?'

'I did. Fferyllt is an ancient word for a timeless group of men; we have always heard it... even when it is whispered many hundreds of miles away.'

'But, it's just a word. A word isn't a person; it can't cry out.'

132

Elis's rasping cough overtook him, as he shook his head. 'You have learnt nothing since you arrived here.'

'I have learnt that you need my help.'

Elis spun around in shock. 'I do not need—'

'I think you do,' The nobleman interrupted, peering down his nose at the druid. 'I think that cough makes you weak. You require my ambition to match to your own. I think that I am your chance to survive!'

A hush descended across the mountains. Even the howling wind beyond the goatskin door stilled. Then, suddenly, Elis laughed, and the gale beyond the dwelling began again. 'Perhaps you *can* learn.' He tapped the twig against the bowl. 'There may yet be a way.'

'A way for what?'

'For us to help each other towards our goals,' Elis replied, averting his eyes from his companion as he plunged the twig back into the bowl. 'You must concentrate. Fully.'

'I will.'

Elis muttered, 'In truth, I wish I did not have to depend on you, dyn drwg, but time is short... and, as you say, your greed is useful to me.'

Not wasting his time on arguing, the nobleman returned to the bowl. 'You were showing me the outlaws asleep in the forest. What must I do?'

'Together we will convince one of *them* to kill the Magic Man.' He swirled the liquid in the bowl once again, keeping to himself the image that had disturbed him. It had been the image of a blond nobleman, a man hounded by conflicting duties... a man shrouded in a mist of future uncertainties, who may or may not heed Herne's calling. A man he feared.

Oblivious to the druid's concerns, his companion stared greedily into the bowl. 'You will be free of your enemy if I can master how to kill via the distance of magic?'

'Quite so dyn drwg,' Elis confirmed. 'So, which outlaw do you choose to carry out our task?'

CHAPTER SIXTEEN

'Wickham first?' Marion asked, as they sorted the food on the wagon into equal shares for each of Sherwood's villages, with the weak rays of early morning sun warming their bones.

'Good idea,' Robin agreed. 'They've been our closest allies for so long.'

'Edward will be pleased,' Little John said, heaving a barrel of ale from one end of the cart to other. 'There, that's one barrel per village—a little extra gift from Abbot Hugo for the trouble he and his brother caused.'

'Only seems right,' Will grinned. 'And one spare for us?'

John patted the barrel he'd placed by the empty cooking pot. 'Seems pretty fair—it's thirsty work all of this, after all. You want to open it up for us, Tuck?'

'No thank you, John.'

'You ain't still going on about this coming from holy ground, are you, Tuck?' Will tutted.

'Just because *you* have no principles, Scarlet.'

Will wrinkled his nose. 'That's true, I don't... especially not when it comes to free ale.'

'That one.'

Elis inclined his head a fraction. 'A wise choice.'

'Now what do we do?'

'We harness his passion, resentment and inner rage. How much easier that will be once he's had some ale.'

The nobleman eagerly took hold of Elis's willow twig and watched the shifting patterns within the bowl before him.

'Where the hell have you been, Gisburne?' The Sheriff blinked into the early morning light as his deputy ran into the abbey's courtyard just as he was mounting his horse, ready to return to Nottingham. 'I had it on good authority that you were dead.'

'You were wrong.' Gisburne glared at his master, asking, 'You knew I was in danger, though?'

'I didn't *know*, but it was suggested you might be.'

'And you did nothing to help me?'

'I sent a guard into the forest. Did he not find you?'

'No.'

'Hmm. Probably thought better of it and ran off,' The Sheriff shrugged. 'You're just in time to escort me to the castle. Where's your horse?'

'Stolen.'

'Really, Gisburne, you can be so careless.'

'Careless? I was almost killed!'

'And yet here you are. I suggest you run along and get another horse fast, or you'll have to be a big brave boy and ride to the castle all on your own.' Robert de Rainault turned to his brother and said, witheringly, 'We are leaving now, Hugo. I look forward to hearing how you'll make it up to me.'

'Make *what* up to you?'

'Losing all my food, of course.'

Hugo's mouth dropped open. For once, his brother's attitude had made him speechless.

'When you have replaced all that's been lost, you'll be welcome at the castle again.'

Finding his voice, Hugo finally said, 'On whose good authority?'

'What?'

'You just told Gisburne here that we heard it on "good authority" that he was dead. You only heard what the Magic Man had to say—what he made me see. Since when was that sort of authority good enough for you?'

The Sheriff sniffed and steered his horse towards the gateway. 'Goodbye, Hugo. Do take care.'

'Are you alright, Tuck?'

'Not really, Little Flower. I can't help thinking that I ought to be helping. I do want the villagers to have their food back, but...'

'It's alright. We understand.'

'Scarlet doesn't.'

'He doesn't want to, that's all.'

'Sometimes I think it might be easier not to believe in anything.'

'I'm sure that, sometimes, Will thinks it would be nice to believe in something bigger than just his trust in us,' Marion said, giving Tuck a hug. 'Why don't you go back to sleep for a bit? It's early. Then, when you awake, you could make us a wonderful stew to return to whilst we're gone?'

'I will. Thank you, Little Flower.'

Waving a hand to his friends as he settled into his favoured sleeping spot, Tuck lay down, his head propped up against a tree, and closed his eyes. 'I'll just have five minutes, and then I'll chop some onions...'

Snoring soon filled the clearing as Tuck drifted into some much-needed sleep, his thoughts full of mutton and cabbage.

'Brother Tuck...'

Tuck gave an extra loud snore, his head lolling to one side against the tree trunk.

'Do not be alarmed... I come to you in sleep to warn you.'

'Warn me,' Tuck muttered, as he slept on.

'He feeds off anger.'

'Who does?'

'Fferyllt.'

Tuck woke with a start, his eyes wide open. He peered around him, but there was no one there. His voice small, he whispered, 'Magic Man?'

'I am in Sherwood... my enemy is near and yet far.'

'Robin isn't here.'

'He is in danger... and one amongst you... I see red...'

Tuck gulped. 'Like blood on bread.'

'Like blood on bread.'

'What can I do?'

'Find your friends. Now.'

'I will.'

'Hurry, Tuck. Hurry. The nature of Herne's Son's future depends upon it.'

'The *nature* of his future? Not his future?' A trickle of dread ran through Tuck as he hurried forwards.

'His followers, his friends... red...'

'And you can take that smirk off your face, John!'

Little John's brow furrowed. 'What on earth has got into you today, Scarlet? You've done nothing

140

but moan since you got up, and you've been getting grumpier by the minute.'

'I had a bad night.' Will ran a hand over his forehead; his palm came away clammy. 'And my mood was not improved in Wickham by seeing you and Meg so bloody happy, when the rest of us—' his eye caught Robin and Marion, hand in hand, and backtracked, '—when *most* of us ain't!'

Keeping pace with Will and John at the head of the cart as they moved further away from Wickham, Much asked, 'Why did you have such a bad night, Will?'

'I don't know, Much!' Scarlet barked at the youngster. 'Why do *you* always have to ask so many bloody questions?'

'You'll cheer up when you see how happy the people in Calverton will be to see their food.'

'I doubt that,' Scarlet said, pinching his forehead between two fingers.

'Have you got a headache, Will?' Marion asked.

'I just said I did, didn't I!' Will bent down, picked up a stick, and threw it hard into the trees. 'What's the point of talking if no one listens?'

'Don't speak to Marion like that!'

'I'll do what I like, thank you very much, John Little.'

Thinking back to the day before, Much mused, 'Wonder if a headache means you're going to get one of them visions like Tuck did, then?'

'Not a chance,' Scarlet grunted. 'Tuck believes in all that stuff; I don't.'

'But Robin has had one too, so…'

'*I ain't Robin!*' Will shouted as he steered the horse that was pulling the wagon around a fallen tree. 'Now, perhaps you can all shut up and let me have my headache in peace?'

'Sorry.'

'Yeah, well, this is all a waste of time anyway.'

Marion gave Will a sidelong glance. 'What do you mean?'

'We're outlaws. We should be keeping the food, not giving it away.'

Little John laid a hand on Much's shoulder as he watched Will. 'We aren't mercenaries.'

'Aren't we? Hah! Get real, John. We are criminals living in a forest. You know it, I know it, Robin knows it. Time we started to admit it.'

Marion threw her friends a worried glance. 'I'm going to catch up with Robin and Nasir.'

'So you can complain about me, I suppose?'

'No, Will. To walk with people who aren't going to bite my head off every time I speak.'

'I'm sure he'll be thrilled to see you,' Will grumbled, scowling at the ground as a level of resentment and fury that he hadn't felt in a long time twisted in his gut like a knife.

'I'm impressed,' Elis muttered, as he huddled over the bowl, 'but you need to push harder, make him turn on his friends.'

The nobleman felt the power of the pool seeping up his arms. 'How?'

'Concentrate on your anger, your resentment, your desires… and make them his.'

'That should not be too difficult,' The nobleman admitted, offering a sly grin.

'I'm sure it won't be. Those qualities make up your very essence,' the druid agreed. He took a ladle from a small rack on the wall and dipped it into the water, the action causing the liquid within the bowl to pool into two halves. 'I will manage the Magic Man; you manage the outlaw.'

CHAPTER SEVENTEEN

Friar Tuck tutted to himself as he left Edward of Wickham. He'd missed his friends by some minutes, and was already tiring.

'More strength, Lord, I must find them,' He said to keep himself going, listening out for trouble along the way. 'The Magic Man *must* have been talking about Will. No one sees red like he does!'

'Herne?'

The Lord of the Trees lowered his antlered cloak from his head, clutching its weight to his chest. 'I thought you would come.'

'Thought or knew?'

'Suspected.' The spirit gestured to the ground. 'Sit with me, Storyteller.'

'I cannot stay long.'

'Indeed, you cannot, for my son will need you.' Herne closed his eyes. 'But I cannot understand how... how I am blocked from seeing him.'

'The druid is strong.'

'Ahh,' Herne exhaled, 'Fferyllt. I saw mountains. I wondered.'

'The very last one.'

Herne placed a palm flat against the tree next to him, taking in strength from the forest itself. 'Elis? After all this time?'

'The stories say he hunted for others who could help him, but no one came to his aid whom he would accept.'

'None were as strong as you.'

'I'm flattered. But he could always have turned to you.'

Herne raised his arms to either side as if to encompass his domain. 'I am bound to Sherwood and cannot leave. I was no use to him here. Elis may be insane—but he is not one for wasting his time.'

'This is true.' The Magic Man began to write in the dirt at his side.

'You seek my help because you cannot fight him alone.'

'He has another with him. Helping him. He has no magic of his own, but borrows the druid's. I can sense his greed.'

'I have felt him too,' Herne confirmed, watching as the Magic Man closed his eyes and continued to write...

Dy...

'Your son and his followers helped me.'

'And you helped them.'

'I did.' Paying no attention to what he was doing, the Magic Man's finger kept writing.

Dyn dr...

'Dyn drwg?'

The Magic Man opened his eyes and looked at what he'd scrawled in the earth.

Dyn drwg.

'So, *he* is the new face in the story.' Herne's solemn expression became graver still as he produced a small flask from the folds of his tunic. He weighed it in his palm. 'We must both drink from this vial.'

The Magic Man took it without question.

As Herne rose to his feet, he asked, 'Will you make this into one of your stories?'

'*Everything* is a future story.'

The horned god replaced his antlers. 'Are you going to tell my son and his friends that the ballads sung about them were whispered into the minds of others by you? That *you* are their chronicler?'

'No. Some things are best left for mankind to wonder about,' the Magic Man said, smiling. '*They* are destined to be the stuff of legend, not me.'

'That they are.' Herne said, lifting the tiny glass flask. 'Once we have drunk this, our thoughts will work together, but the strength of my mind is all I can give. Any more and he'll know I'm aiding you... and my son's life will be in even more danger than it is already.'

'Understood,' the Magic Man replied as he watched the Lord of the Trees remove the stopper. 'Together, we shall defeat the ones who need to hide far away.'

Herne tilted his head back and drank. Instantly, his body stilled. 'It is time. Elis wants you to go and find Robin.'

'Yes. I must do what Elis wants... so he doesn't *get* what he wants.'

'It is the only way to fight the one who isn't there,' Herne stated, lifting his eyes to the canopy of leaves above him. 'Hurry. I see red...'

'How *dare* you,' Will Scarlet shouted as he smacked a fist onto the side of the wagon, 'I would never steal from the villagers. Never!'

'I saw you,' Robin countered.

Will Scarlet's face burned a deep red with indignation. 'You couldn't have seen me, because I didn't do anything.'

'What's in your pocket, then?' Robin demanded, squaring up to Will with his hands on his hips.

'I didn't put anything in my—' Scarlet faltered as, pulling his hand back out of the offending pocket, he produced some onions. He seemed genuinely shocked as he muttered, 'How did *they* get there?'

'Don't play the innocent with me,' Robin snapped. 'You've been acting like an angry boar since we got to Wickham, and goodness knows what the people of Claverton think of you after you were rude to pretty much everyone there. What's the matter with you?'

Interrupting any reply his friend might have made, a confused Much asked, 'What you want onions for, Will?'

'I *don't* want 'em! I'd take apples if I was taking anything... which I ain't. Someone else put 'em there.'

'And who would have done that?' Robin asked.

'You! You're always having a go at me. Maybe you wanted to get rid of me once and for all? Accusing me of stealing is a great excuse.'

Marion stepped between the men, shouting, 'Stop it! We do *not* have time for this. We have more food to deliver. Come on.'

'Not until whoever put them onions in my pocket owns up!' Scarlet cried, rounded on John. 'I bet it was you. You're tall enough to creep up on me, and—'

'I did no such thing, lad!'

Will circled on the spot, looking from one outlaw to the other. Unconsciously, his hand went to his knife. He had drawn it before he knew what he was doing. 'Keep away from me, all of you!'

Alarmed now, the other outlaws backed away.

'You've had it in for me since we left camp. I've had enough!'

'No,' Little John yelled. '*You've* been in a foul mood since—'

'I have not!' Without warning, Will launched himself at John, knife gripped tight in his hand.

'Will, stop!' cried Robin as the two friends wrestled, one trying hard to avoid the knife of the other without hurting him at the same time.

'Do something, Robin!' Marion shrieked, watching in horror as John only just managed to dodge a blow from Will's blade.

Elis glowered into his half of the bowl. 'The Magic Man is coming.'

The nobleman smiled as he watched the chaos unfolding in his part of the vision. 'They fight… but they don't know why.'

'Keep concentrating,' The druid ordered, clutching his willow twig, 'soon this will be over.'

'And the Hooded Man shall come to the forest…'

The Magic Man closed his eyes, trusting his own instinct with the help of Herne's mind to guide him.

As he walked through Sherwood, lines he'd written, spoken, and sung before passed in front of his eyes; there were a litany of stories, of threads to the past, the present and the future... all ready to be pulled, knotted or remembered. Words Herne had spoken, Robin Hood had spoken, his enemies had spoken... or words they would one day speak. Events he would turn into stories, magic he would weave that would enchant the tale for eternity.

The Silver Arrow is mine...

'That's the past.'

He walked faster.

Run, Robin... Run, damn you...

'The future... another's future... Herne's Son, but not yet Herne's Son.'

The Magic Man began to run.

The Hunter shall become the hunted...

'Timeless... a phrase for eternity...'

He opened his eyes and his run became a sprint.

'Look out!' Tears welled up in Much's eyes, as Will tried again to stab Little John, the giant man again only just able to roll out of reach of the expertly-aimed blade in the nick of time. 'Why are they fighting? I don't understand.'

'Stop!' Robin ordered again, but Will Scarlet was not for stopping.

'I've never seen him like this,' Marion said, her face pale as helplessly she witnessed the brawl before them. 'Will's face is red... even his eyes are...'

'They're scarlet,' Robin gasped. 'He's bewitched! He must be. Why didn't I see it before?'

'But who would—'

'The Magic Man,' Nasir spat through gritted teeth, pulling a knife from his belt. 'Shall I throw it?'

'Are you sure you can hit Will and not John?'

'As sure as I can be, Robin,' the Saracen said, frowning. 'I do not like this.'

'Nor do I,' Marion replied, shaking her head. 'You can't stab Will, Nasir!'

'But if he's been possessed, we *need* to stop him before he kills John,' Robin stated, blowing out a gust of breath in frustration. 'I'm going to stop them.'

'How? Look at them,' Marion asked, gripping hold of Robin's arm. 'It's impossible.'

'I have to try.'

My name was Scathlock, it's Scarlet now...

'Past. His past... red.'

The Magic Man's chest constricted with fatigue as he continued to pound through the forest, stories on his lips.

I'd die for each and every one of you...

'Future. His future... if I can get there in time... if I can ensure he *has* a future.'

For the first time in his life, Robin found himself wishing that Scarlet wasn't so skilled with a knife. He tried to catch John's eye as the bigger man rolled to the left, once again only just escaping a serious wound.

Edging from side to side, trying to stay behind the fighters, Robin watched the flash of the blade as it danced, agile in Will's palm, waiting for his chance.

At last, Little John noticed Robin, and just as Scarlet threw back his arm to drive the blade into his friend's shoulder, he let out a roar, 'Now!'

Diving forwards, Robin grasped Will's shoulders and yanked him backwards, just as John lunged a hand forwards, his fist on target to hit his attacker's chin. But a split second before it made contact, Scarlet swerved to the right, and John's punch met Robin's shoulder, sending him flying backwards.

Rushing to a dazed Robin's side, Much, Marion and Nasir held their collective breath as they continued to watch their friends fight. Will was silent now as he focused on beating his rival. They rolled this way and that, evenly matched in every way as they exchanged blows and dodged punches, Little John always needing to avoid Scarlet's blade.

Marion whispered, 'Why would the Magic Man do this?'

'I don't know,' Robin replied, massaging his shoulder. Readying himself to try and stop the fight for a second time, he added, 'Tuck wouldn't believe it was him, and I'm not sure I do... but *someone* has got into Will's mind.'

'The visions the Magic Man was having; Tuck said someone was affecting them,' Marion remembered, grabbing hold of Robin's arm. 'What if *they've* got to Will? What if—' She broke off, turning swiftly. 'Someone's coming!'

Robin drew his bow as he, Marion, Much and Nasir dived into the trees.

CHAPTER EIGHTEEN

'Tuck!' Marion let out a sigh of relief. 'That's the second time you've appeared out of nowhere and made us jump this week. I do wish you'd...' Her words floated into fresh air as the friar barrelled straight past them and on towards where John and Will were grappling.

'What on earth...' Robin went to run after Tuck, but he faltered as another figure appeared on the far side of the fighters. 'The Magic Man!'

Much drew the slingshot from his pocket. 'Should I load it, Robin? I could fire it at him.'

'Load it just in case, Much, but don't fire unless I say so.'

No sooner had Robin spoken than they heard Tuck call, 'John! Roll now!'

The second Tuck spoke, Robin, Nasir, Much and Marion darted forwards, just in time to see John give a massive heave, pushing both of his arms forwards and knocking Scarlet off him. The Magic Man also came running at full speed towards them.

'You?' cried Will. Swerving to the right, he instantly lost any interest he'd had in hurting John; leaping to his feet, he hurtled at full pelt towards the Magic Man.

'Scarlet, no!' Tuck puffed, his legs working with a speed and determination that he knew would cost him later.

As Will reached the Magic Man, he threw his arm back, blade ready to strike.

'*No!*' Not stopping to consider that he might get hurt himself, Tuck barrelled into Will, sending him sprawling to the left. Propelled forwards by his own weight and speed, the friar then collided with the Magic Man, knocking them both to the ground.

Elis dropped the twig. 'What's happened? Why aren't they moving?' He tore his gaze from the pool, demanding, 'What did you do?'

'Nothing.' Confused and frustrated, the nobleman kept his eyes on the drama unfolding on the surface of the sapphire liquid. 'He should have stabbed the Storyteller... he should have—'

'But he didn't! And now he can't.' Elis shook his head hard. 'I don't see his mind... the Magic Man must be unconscious.'

'That's good... isn't it?'

'Good? How can I control his mind if he isn't conscious? You fool! I needed him awake or dead— dead for preference! We were so close. And now I must start again, just because you couldn't make one hothead stab someone!'

Rage filled the nobleman. 'I did all I was told. And you shared no real information; I didn't know what to do. I came here for help, but all you've done is exploit me to get what *you* wanted! You never had any intention of helping me rise to power, did you?'

'I showed you the people you need to deal with! I gave you a chance to see—'

The nobleman's gloved fist hit Elis full in the face. 'You have given me nothing! Just like everyone before you. I'm worthy of so much more than this!'

Elis made a grab for the willow twig, but this time his companion was faster.

'No! I've had enough—you played me.'

The crack of the willow as the noble bent the twig over his knee, breaking it into two even pieces, was drowned out by Elis's scream. It was a scream that bounced off the stone walls, escaped through the goatskin doorway and ricocheted through the mountains.

The Magic Man's eyes flew open and he sat bolt upright. 'He's dead.'

'And you're not... thank God!' Tuck said as he crossed himself. 'You had me worried for a minute.'

Will glanced anxiously towards Little John, who was having his black eye and a growing collection of bruises tended to by Marion. 'What the hell happened?'

'You were being controlled by a druid; his name is Elis,' the Magic Man explained.

'Never 'eard of 'im.'

'You wouldn't have. He belongs to a different story.'

Scarlet winced as he flexed his arm, bruises of his own making themselves apparent. 'Robin said I was possessed.'

'You were, in a way. It's more that he harnessed your inner resentments and used them against you to get what he wanted.'

Robin frowned, 'And what he wanted was for Will to kill you.'

'Yes,' agreed the Magic Man. 'He needed me to keep the Fferyllt going, to keep *himself* going. When I refused to help him, he decided that I must die.'

'How did *he* die? We didn't kill him; he's not even here,' Much enquired, puzzled.

'You must fight one who isn't there,' Robin said, nodding slowly. 'Herne said that to me before we went to the abbey. This druid; he isn't here... and yet we had to help you fight him.'

'And with Herne's aid, we did.'

'*Herne* helped?' Marion looked around, half expecting to see the spirit appear before them.

'He lent his strength to my own—without it, I would not have seen the words I needed to see.'

'I don't understand,' Will said, massaging the back of his neck.

'You don't need to. What matters is that we took his story and changed its ending.'

Robin studied their guest. 'And the powerful man who died; that was this druid?'

'A victim of his own magic.'

'His magic, or yours?'

'His combined with another's; an untrained avarice whom he could not control.' Standing up, the Magic Man placed a hand on Tuck's shoulder. 'Thank you, good friar. You saved me today.'

'You saved yourself.'

'Too kind.' He bowed, before turning to Will. 'Are you alright now, Scathlock?'

'Yes, I—' Will looked more closely at the dishevelled man, who's hazel eyes were now filled with kindness, and queried, 'How did you know Scathlock was my name?'

'I heard it in a story.'

'Did you now?'

'Oh yes.'

Will thought for a second, before asking, 'Why me? Why not one of the others?'

The Magic Man laid a hand on Will's arm and closed his eyes. 'I will tell you privately.'

'Privately?' Will was about to get up so they could move away from the others, when he heard the Magic Man's voice in his head.

'*You were chosen because you wear your emotions openly. Anger, pain, hurt... they can all be exploited by those who seek to do harm. They choose you, Will Scarlet, because you are the one who has survived the*

160

most horror, making you both the bravest and the most vulnerable of them all.'

'Oh.'

'And your story will last forever.'

Not sure what to say, and wanting to avoid the anxious and inquisitive looks of his friends, Will simply mumbled, 'Right, thanks. At least that's over with then. Story told.'

The Magic Man opened his eyes and smiled. 'Story told.'

'Thank you.'

'You are very welcome.' The Magic Man got to his feet. 'And now, I must go. There are stories to tell, and a living to make.'

'You're a minstrel, then?' Much looked at the man in surprise. 'We had one of them here once, Alan a Dale. Do you know him?'

'I have heard of him, yes,' the Magic Man replied, smiling at the echo of a story he'd once imagined. 'But no, I'm no minstrel. I cannot sing.'

'Neither could he,' Much confided.

'I simply tell stories; sometimes they help people.'

'How?'

'They make them smile; they help them forget— just for a little while—how hard life can be. I try to give hope, laughter… joy…'

Robin smiled, 'A noble thing to do.'

'Thank you, Herne's Son.'

Tuck tilted his head to one side. 'You didn't tell me your name... your *real* name.'

'I didn't, did I,' the Magic Man admitted as he winked. 'It's Richard... although many a year has passed since I was addressed as such. My friends call me Kip.'

Much edged a little closer to their new friend, noting that his clothing somehow looked less ragged than it had before. 'What are your stories about, Kip?'

'Life. Hope. Survival. They're about people like you.'

'Oh.'

'Life, you say?' Robin stretched out a hand for the storyteller to shake. 'A big subject, life. How do you remember it all?'

'I just do.'

'You must have an excellent memory.'

'Nothing's forgotten, Robin Hood. Nothing is ever forgotten.'

EPILOGUE

He stumbled through the mountains, his eyes half closed against the freezing, falling snow.

The druid is dead.

'Dead?' Panic seized him. He really was alone. 'But all I did was break the twig.'

It held his life, his power. Without it, his magic was gone.

'It was just a stick.'

And you are just a man, yet look what damage you have caused by playing with magic.

The nobleman span around, terror nudging at his ribs. 'I'll die here alone.'

You are not alone... I am here. I will guide you, but...

'Let me guess... for a price?'

No. For a promise.

Holding his cloak around him, grateful for the black gloves he always wore—but fearing even they wouldn't be enough to stop his fingers from freezing off if he didn't reach the foot of the mountains soon—he snapped, 'Who are you? *Where* are you?'

In the forest you will come to despise.

'Which forest?'

You will learn that when it is time for that chapter of your story to be read.

A tiny spark of hope lit a warmth in his chest. 'Then I live?'

It is not yet your time to die.

'You will lead me out of here?'

For a promise.

'Oh, go on then! But hurry. I'm cold.'

You will leave witchcraft to those who know how to use it fairly.

He scoffed, agreement ready on his lips. 'That I can promise freely! I've had enough of all of it! Now, get me down from here.'

An abrupt peace coated the mountains. The wind had stopped, the snow gone.

You got yourself there, you must get yourself down... but the path is now clear.

'You promised you'd get me down!'

164

I broke my promise... just as you will break yours.

'I will not! I said that I never want to meddle in magic again. Ever.'

We will see.

Shivering—but no longer freezing—the man stumbled forwards as a haphazard path appeared. He followed it; walking, scrabbling, sliding, downwards.

It was only after several hours—his hands bleeding, his limbs aching, his back sore—that he had enough breath to whisper, 'I deserve so much more than this.'

You will get what you deserve.

Startled, he saw a man stood on the path before him. He wore simple, faded green clothing, with no cloak to keep him warm. His brown hood was down, despite the cold; his grey hair framed a haggard face half-covered by a straggly beard.

'Who are you? Where did you come from?'

'Do you not recognise me?'

He screwed up his eyes. 'I... yes... you were in the visions. But that was Nottinghamshire, and this is... How did you—'

'So many questions, my Lord.'

'My Lord?' He stepped back. 'The druid would not address me thus.'

'The druid lied to you about many things.'

'I know,' the nobleman replied, a shifting sensation running through him. 'He had no reason to. I was going to help him.'

'Do you still intend to kill me, now you have destroyed Elis?'

He shuffled his feet. 'You truly are the one he wanted me to kill? The Magic Man.'

'I am.'

'I did not know breaking the willow would end him.'

'I don't think he did either. He lived too long, put too much of himself into his magic,' the Magic Man sighed. 'So, are you going to end me too?'

Face to face with the man with the shining hazel eyes, the nobleman reached for his sword, but found himself hesitating.

'It's not like you to waver over the death of someone you consider inferior to yourself.'

His hand on the hilt of his sword, the nobleman asked, 'Do you know who I am?'

'Oh yes, you are part of the story.'

'Whose story?'

'Your own, of course. And his. Theirs... There are two of them.'

'Two?'

'Oh yes, there are two. One dark-haired, one blond. Both living in the realm of light, but battling the dark.'

'Dark, light; light, dark… you make no sense,' said the nobleman, shaking his head and thrusting his sword back into his belt. He pushed past the man and trudged onwards, only looking back to say, 'I see no point in murdering you for a dead druid who never kept his word.'

'Take the left path, dyn drwg, and you'll reach the village. Take the right and the town will greet you. Either way, the remainder of your life will find you.'

Taking no comfort from this, he stopped in his tracks, staring at the choice of trackways that ran off to either side. Looking back again, he asked, 'Why did the druid call me "dyn drwg"?'

'It is a fitting title, my Lord.'

'But my title is…'

'Oh I know what your title is,' the Magic Man smiled. 'Dyn drwg means *bad man*. If you are lucky, you could earn a new name. There is still time for you to change, to be a good person who helps others.'

The noble's humourless laugh cracked the crisp air as he stroked his dark goatee, and a sardonic half-smile played over his features. 'How dare Elis give me that name!' he cried out, against the wind.

The Magic Man's image began to fade.

'Come back! Take me with you! I want to get out of here. The paths are too long, it's so cold, and...'

Herne passed the Magic Man a drink. 'Here, this will help you recover from your projection.'

The Magic Man bowed. 'Thank you.'

Herne pressed his hands against the cave's altar. 'And now we wait.'

'Will he be become a better man, do you think?'

'It is too soon to tell. But,' the Lord of the Trees sighed, 'I fear that within Lord Edgar of Huntingdon, the poison already runs too deep.'

Also from Chinbeard and Oak Tree Books

Richard Carpenter's
ROBIN OF SHERWOOD

THE
HELL MOUTH

John Semper

You may also enjoy...

NOTHING'S FORGOTTEN...

In May 2014, I put on the 30th anniversary Robin of Sherwood convention, a huge celebration of our beloved series, at the St. Pierre in Chepstow, England. We fired flaming arrows, we ate a banquet, we had a medieval encampment and archery contests, and the two Robins appeared on stage together for the first time ever in front of an audience. The fans turned out in their hundreds, and I continued putting on events until the 40th anniversary celebration in November 2024, at the British Film Institute.

My ethos was simple, to make people laugh and to connect the love that the fans have for the show with the love the cast and crew have for the show. I can honestly say, the decade I've poured into keeping the flaming arrow in the air, to enhance (and never extinguish) the legacy, has been an emotional journey.

Alongside the events, I became the accidental producer of Robin of Sherwood, when I was left to solely finish 'The Knights of the Apocalypse' (the full-cast audio 'movie' of the unproduced feature-length script by Richard 'Kip' Carpenter). From there, I produced and directed new adventures on audio and commissioned (and sometimes wrote) new and official stories in book form.

It took a lot of time and dedication to negotiate the licenses (there's more than one!), to be able to continue 'Robin of Sherwood', and my delight at being able to gift one back to Richard Carpenter's Estate (due to my deep delve into paperwork and archive legalities) means that they now have the literary license to allow others to use it. It took nearly 30 years for the show to be resurrected and I'm very proud that I managed to make it happen.

I've been helped along the way by the support of the fans, the support of the cast and crew of the show, and talented chums like Iain Meadows and Jennifer Ash (including all the other writers, sound designers, composers, artists, graphic designers, formatters, editors, and recording studios).

None of this would have been achieved without the counsel of Harriet Whitehouse, the daughter of Kip. She has been a steadfast rock of moral and mental support, as well as a keen eye for what works and what doesn't in the stories we told.

Spiteful Puppet and AUK Studios have also been a rock, in allowing these adventures to see the light of day, with particular mention going out to Paul Andrews for allowing me to get to the end of the licenses I had, to create all of this.

The fans have kept the show alive and are the true beating heart of Sherwood, with fan fiction, previous events, fan clubs, internet forums, and their unwavering belief that this is the seminal version of the Robin Hood tale. And I bask in their light and thank each and every one of you who has bought a ticket, a book, an audio, or just wished me well from afar.

But, of course, the true Herne, the true guiding spirit, is Richard 'Kip' Carpenter – the writer and creator of Robin of Sherwood. I always did my best to think like he thought, write like he wrote, and be protective of his vision. Even when others disagreed or seemed not to understand how the show ticked.

I had the idea of 'The Magic Man' a while back, knowing I wanted to bow out after a decade of being allowed to play in his sandbox. The idea of a storyteller whose vision and words affected the past and the future, whose story was compromised by dark forces, and how the magic of words can heal, wound, soothe, excite, damage, or inspire, almost came fully formed. I knew I wanted this storyteller to be controlled by a villain from the television series and – as I often do with previous books and audios – I roughly wrote a treatment of how the tale would pan out. I'd often do this and leave other writers to embellish my ideas (and create something of their own from my initial thoughts).

For 'The Magic Man', I simply ran out of time to write the book myself, so I turned to Jennifer Ash (who has written the majority of the stories in the last decade) and we bashed our heads together to come up with something suitably epic from my scribblings. Something that would be a fitting finale, in the form of an original tale, that linked in with the show and paid homage to its writer and creator. I had always wanted to dedicate it 'For Kip…', because – without whom – all of this wouldn't exist.

I think, and I hope you do too, that's it's possibly mine and Jennifer's best work. I adore this tale, and I thank Jennifer so much for giving all of herself to it, to help me create one last tale for Kip.

It's been a long journey through Sherwood.

I've encountered mostly love but I've also encountered a fair bit of hate, fighting, and backstabbing at the beginning and at the end (the middle bit was rather soft and romantic). Such is the way with adventure stories!

But I now take off my fake antlers and back away into the dry ice, as Clannad hauntingly plays in the background. I was a mere inconsequential cog in the massive engine of this legendary show, just a conduit for the fans and the cast to meet, greet, and (in some cases) fall in love and wed!

I hope, if I've met you, you've enjoyed my company and had your heart lifted a little by what I've managed to achieve over these last ten years. If not, I'm sorry! You can't please everyone!!

But, although I'll be forgotten, the show won't.

And nor will Kip.

Shine on.

Best wishes & rainbow fishes,
Barnaby Eaton-Jones

Richard Carpenter's
ROBIN OF SHERWOOD

THE KNIGHTS OF
THE APOCALYPSE

Richard Carpenter
with Barnaby Eaton-Jones